AFTERMATH

CURVE

OF

HUMANITY

BOOK FIVE

MAQUEL A. JACOB

Cover art by:

Keith Johnston

https://keithdraws.wordpress.com

Edited by:

Rhiannon Rhys-Jones

Published by MAJart Works

www.majartworks.com

Hillsboro, Oregon

©Copyright 2018

ISBN: 978-1-950438-93-8

ACKNOWLEDGEMENTS

Thank you for tackling book five in the Curve of Humanity series. Only one left to wrap it. My one goal is to find the good in humanity and show we can combat corruption within our hearts and society. This series is a lesson of hope in the face of futility.

For this world to change, we must also.

For those who encouraged me to keep going when it all seemed too daunting, I appreciate you all. A huge thanks to NaNoWriMo (National Novel Writing Month) for supporting writers' creative juices. My peeps at NIWA, you all keep my humble and showed me to put myself out there with no fear.

To my awesome editor Rhiannon Rhys Jones. You are a treasure. You keep me on my toes and force me to constantly up my game. Thank you, William F. Nolan for constantly telling me not to quit; to keep writing and keep learning.

Keith Johnston: Your talent is mind blowing. I never thought the covers would turn out so amazing. Can't wait to work with you again on future projects.

CHAPTER ONE

A Sonnet for Humanity

-Blind Sheep-

I had hope for some sense of sanity
It being the 21st century of man
But, it seems we are losing our humanity
With no way of fixing it- If we can.
The end is near, or so they say
They, being the prophets and pessimists
Salivating at the promise of doomsday
Even as society and everyday life persists.
Let us not fall in line
Marching towards our own annihilation
And read into the inevitable sign
Of our final destination
Lest we forget an important note
We all wear the same human coat.

- Rachel E. Robinson 2012

SURVIVAL OF THE FITTEST

Dark shadows cascaded across the dimly lit walls inside the bunker. Eighteen men and women wrapped in makeshift tattered ponchos were huddled on the floor under blankets to keep warm. The temperature in the bunker dropped to fifty degrees for six hours every day. Too short for night and happened at random times. One of the men adjusted the thermal blanket covering himself and the person on either side of him. They were strangers at the start. Each one an expert in their respective science field.

The only one in the room standing, head bowed down over a metal table was Professor Heines. Still clinging to some symbol of professionalism, he wore a white lab coat that had seen better days over a pair of green scrubs. The others had adopted the same attire when conducting tests in the lab. His short hair was cut crudely, and his beard was trimmed to a decent length. There would be no rescue but just in case, he wanted to appear sane.

When the last transport to evacuate Earth landed for loading during the battle, an urge to see it through came over him. At the last moment, he backed away and headed to the nearest bunker along with the other sadists. He had taken the reins as lead scientist of the small group due to his level head when everyone else went into a panic, scared of their chances for survival even this far underground.

It all went south after they felt the impact of an enemy blast. He could tell by the way the bunker seemed to tilt nearly ninety degrees before settling back down, not quite level, that the ground had lifted all around them. Anything above on the outside would not have survived, he was sure of that. The bunker maintaining its integrity was a miracle. Over time, it shifted. Not quite flat; though close enough.

On the other side of the bunker was a small lab to do their research. When all the work was done, there was nothing left to do except wait for the next round of specimens. Heines kept morale up with his optimism. He would constantly talk about how Earth would bounce back and flourish. History had already shown the planet could sustain major damage and still thrive. Of course, that depended on humans having learned their lesson and not repeat their mistakes.

Every three months a group of scouts were sent out with equipment to gauge the air quality and test the soil. They would return within five to eight days depending on how the weather topside was acting. It was the only thing keeping the small group from killing each other. Moments of hostility followed by mental breakdowns were common events, yet they forced themselves through it. Their faces were weary from being on endless watch rotation while they waited for the last crew of explorers to come back. To revert to caveman mentality in the face of adversity was not an option.

After five years, Earth appeared to have gotten better. Two years earlier it was still not up to livable conditions. The rain that started two months prior brought more despair, turning what soil remained black like soot. Early test samples showed nothing could grow in it.

One of the specimen cubes sitting beside him on the metal table lit up alerting to a test finishing. A female scientist wiggled herself out of the huddle and crossed the room to check on it, passing Heines. She adjusted her glasses then pulled down on her wrinkled scrubs top.

"Is that the soil specimen you modified last month?" Heines asked.

She squinted into the clear containment searching for some signs of success before answering. Her prescription had long expired and her eyesight had certainly deteriorated.

"Yes. I figured we had nothing to lose by trying out a new strain."

"What's the verdict?"

Some of the other scientists seemed to perk up, bracing for it.

"Change in consistency. It looks like crumbled tar now. I guess that's as close to dirt as we're going to get."

"Any growth?"

The female scientist pursed her lips and shook her head. The others deflated back into their huddles. Heines felt the same. The moment anything started to grow, they could focus on farming edible food. With the drastic change of the surface, he wasn't sure what would start coming out of the ground first.

A click from above echoed and they all looked up to see the hatch creak open. In the beginning it would silently slide, its hydraulics working as designed, the sleek metal glinting from the slightest amount of light. Now, it was corroded from the elements. Some days the hatch wouldn't open, having been partially buried as a result from a storm. Dents, scratches, and discoloration covered the outside. The harsh squeal and popping from worn out parts grated on the group's senses. Muted light shone into the bunker revealing swirls of fine dust.

"We made it!" The first person to climb down the metal ring stairs exclaimed. "It's crazy looking out there."

Professor Heines stepped away from the table and met them halfway. The crewman brushed off his battered flak suit and lifted the crusty goggles from his face to set them atop his head.

"What's it like now?" Heines asked.

The second person coming down leapt from the third to the last rung and answered.

"The sky is shades of pink, orange, and grey. Kind of beautiful. The ground is shit though. That black stuff is still everywhere. Not a hint of plant life to be found."

"That rain is nothing nice either," the last in the group said as they climbed down.

"Did you get a new sample?" Heines held out a hand in anticipation.

"Right here," the third replied, handing him a vial. "Also got a few pictures." They turned to the rest of the scientists, waving a battered tablet. "You know how we like our proof of life photos."

The rest of the bunker group stirred from under their blankets and began to rise. Professor Heines inserted the vial into the water tester and hit the process button. Everyone hovered around it, waiting for the result while looking through the new round of images on the tablet. Drinkable water had become scarce on the planet. Most of the oceans were half their size while rivers, lakes and streams had evaporated. What body of water they did find came from the torrential rain and needed to go through a ten step filtration system. Even then, the water had an odd taste and some people broke out in hives.

As luck would have it, they encountered an aquafer some weeks ago and had to haul out portable drilling equipment to access it. The process took longer due to the drill's size and limited depth. Which proved deep enough to pierce the crust so they could extract the liquid gold inside. If the water was at least ten percent better in quality, they could drop down to a five step process and eliminate most of the impurities.

The machine beeped twenty minutes later. Previous and new data flashed side by side on the digital screen showing a seventy two percent improvement. They all burst out with joy, some hugging each other. Professor Heines slowly raised his head and stared at the ceiling.

They would have decent water within the next few weeks.

The third crewman in the exploration crew cleared his throat to get their attention. Heines stepped away from the group and turned to him.

"What is it?"

"Well," they side eyed his partners who seemed to stiffen. "We found something else."

The other scientists stopped their celebration, hearing the ominous tone in his voice. Heines' eyes narrowed.

"There was another group of explorers roaming around."

"Yeah," the first scout said. "They had a weird insignia on their suits"

"Like they were super organized," the second scout added.

That made Heines frown. Other survivors going out to check on the lay of the land was one thing. He expected no less. There were hints of small towns erected farther out but he made sure to stress not going for a peek. Now, he wondered if it was time to explore deeper.

"What style would you say?" Heines finally asked.

The first scout tapped the bottom of his lips then snapped his fingers.

"They reminded me of those Hazmat teams from the CDC. Here." He grabbed the tablet and scrolled through the images to one showing the men in suits.

Government? Heines yelled inside his head.

"You thinking what we're all thinking?" The female scientist asked.

Heines nodded. He went to the far wall and pushed on the corner side panel. A digital keypad appeared, and he typed in a code. Thin lines formed in the shape of a door and recessed before sliding to the right, leaving a dark entrance. He hit the console on the other side and lights flooded the area. Four advanced terrain vehicles sat lined up in the sparse hub. The walls were covered with inactive gauges.

"Oh my god!" The first scout exclaimed. "This has been here the whole time?"

"Well that's just shitty," one of the other scientists said. "We could have covered way more ground over the years."

"Really?" Heines snapped. "And when we lost them due to the unexpected, what then? The ground was not stable until only a couple of years ago. I was biding time. If things got well enough for us to venture out, this was an option."

"You still could have told us," another scientist muttered.

"No! He couldn't." One of the scouts answered. "The way we were going, having meltdowns and shit, one of us would have taken these and caused more chaos."

The man's mouth turned downward, and he gave Heines a dirty look. It was short lived as he noticed his colleagues nodding in agreement.

"We take one out and see how it goes. I still want us to avoid any of those pop up territories." Heines tapped an icon on the touch pad and the gauges on the wall lit up.

"Yeah, for all we know, they could be something out of those post apocalypse movies from the twentieth century. No thank you," another scientist interjected.

"And watch for those other explorers. It doesn't sit well." Everyone nodded. "Now, who's next on rotation? We need you to go out in the next eight days to get more water and find out our true location. For all we know, we could have been carried out hundreds of miles."

In an underground unit the size of a small town the exiled elite had procured before the war, the masses mulled around. A scouting unit had been established and sent out every quarter to determine if it was safe to go topside. Each sector exchanged their findings to different groups. Dirty rainfall had stopped its continuous daily assault three years ago and a new dawn had surfaced.

With the ability to make clean water now wide-spread with the finding of deep reservoirs known as aquafers, survivors began to make bigger communities on the surface. Except them. Going above ground to create a society without a clear plan was suicide.

Three former world leaders had taken control of the underground town two years after the battle between Earth and the Relliants and were close to devising a plan to get all those already topside in line. They were derived from each faction of the former governments so everyone in the town had a voice in the decision making.

The first was a former military commander named Reinhart. His two associates were Professor Omar, a renowned scientist, and Ambassador Jankowski; the former diplomat. Together they ruled with an iron fist in the guise of compassion. All to keep the masses in check and not think too much about getting out. Images taken by the scouts of the nearby settlements made them cringe.

A new world order was needed.

Handfuls of military and world leaders along with a group of scientists had rejected the call to evacuate. The worst offenders of the previous regime in the underground sector banded together for a unified agenda. Even with the planet in shambles, barely recovering, the only thing on their minds was to seize power. The three men had appointed themselves as in charge then went through ruthless methods to make sure accurate data from the surface was collected.

By any means necessary. The order every day.

They took their daily stroll around the sector and took in the situation. The confined space had become hostile as the inhabitants grew tired of being in close quarters with each other. The new leaders went around encouraging them to press on, citing a remedy was near. Safe rooms had been built in anticipation of people going insane, giving them a place to calm down and reset. Until they could seize more territory, the town was their main base.

The three men came upon the commons area and crossed over into an isolated white cube with frosted walls on the front they used for their meetings to minimize prying eyes. A high table sat in the center with four chairs, along with a counter along the wall accompanied by bolted down bar stools. There was also a chaise lounge sitting further in behind the table. All pure white, like the inside. Reinhart sat down in the chaise and stretched out.

"Once the environment cooperates, we will have to find out how many survivors are out there. A true census is key to our success."

Omar walked to the far end of the room and leaned against the wall. He nodded before speaking.

"I'm sure there will be some resistance to change. We need to give them an incentive."

"For what?" Jankowski huffed. "We're all lucky to be alive. That said, there has to be some organization in place."

"Get society back on track. Establish community and trade," Reinhart said.

"I'm sure that's what every human who survived wants," Omar added.

"And the aliens and hybrids?" Reinhart asked

There was a long silence as the three men contemplated individually.

"I don't think it matters, at this point. We're all in the same boat," Omar finally said.

"We should prepare for the worst," Reinhart stated.

"What do you mean?" Jankowski asked.

"You've seen those horrid post apocalyptic movies from the late twentieth and early twenty first century. That could be what's out there. A lot of the information brought back confirms there are a few territories like that."

"We can deal with that," Reinhart spat. "We have a damn arsenal with us and the locations for more if necessary."

"Unless they found them first."

Omar traced circles on the white table as he stared at the wall before him. He had set a small chip on the table and an updated map of the area glowed on its surface.

"Let's tackle that when the time comes. One of our scouts detected a strong energy signature during his investigation. For now, we need to find out where it's coming from."

"Yes," Jankowski sneered. "That signature could only be one thing."

"A facility." Reinhart finished the thought.

Brows furrowed; their expressions grew dark. During the last stages of the evacuation all the world leaders were informed of the facilities locking down, some plunging into the deep depths of the ocean, refusing to engage in the fight. Facilities had advanced technology not known to the public, and the New World Order needed a communications network. If whoever was running that facility didn't offer it up willingly, they would take it by force.

"Spread the word," Reinhart ordered. "We seek out the facilities and any other sections that may have advance capabilities." He tapped the image on the table. It zoomed in on a spot marked with a red symbol indicating the energy source. "Which one are you?"

⤚

The scout crawled up to the edge of the hillside, view goggles attached to his face, and zoomed in on the small patch of single story buildings with string lights around them. People roamed along the narrow pathways. Each shelter was made of metal scraps salvaged from fallen battle ships. The insignias were still visible on a few with scorch marks covering them. Taut lines filled with pieces of clothing ran across the tops connecting the corners of the shelters.

A trio consisting of two men and one female moved with purpose down the alley, shoving women and children on the verge of starvation out of the way. They wore a range of bone necklaces, leather attire and war paint on their faces. It was just as Omar had predicted. Straight out of one of those films from the previous era. There were other small groups like them scattered throughout the region and the scout assumed they were patrols.

He zoomed in a bit more and saw they also had weapons. Makeshift, from what looked like damaged and discarded weapons, but no less dangerous. As proof, one of the men shot a crate of goods for fun. The crate exploded, sending mush flying everywhere.

A waste of food.

The three laughed and continued their stroll. When he turned to the left, he saw a lookout tower sitting low on the edge of the town and cursed. A man with similar goggles was staring right at him. As the man gave a rotten tooth grin, he raised a small cylinder to his lips and blew into it. A loud shrill permeated the air and all the leather clad hordes within the town stopped what they were doing.

The scout hurried the fifty yards back to his transport. He climbed in, engaged the engine and hit the thrusters at full. From the rearview camera, he could see a line of vehicles already giving chase.

Shit that was fast.

The only way they could have mobilized so quickly was if they were already locked and loaded. There were obviously a few areas he couldn't see from his scouting position. He took a good look at their gear. Modified transporters with weapons mounted on the hoods. The glowing amber of the lead vehicle's cannon made him swerve to evade the shot. It hit the ground close to the transport, sending it careening sideways. Not willing to give up yet, he switched the controls to manual and corrected the vehicle's trajectory.

Up ahead was the portable command center fully equipped with land to air combat weapons. Pristine and white, it stood out like a sore thumb. Technicians scattered around working on equipment turned to the sound of his approach. The scout hit the thrusters for more output and widened the distance between himself and his pursuers.

As he sped into the command center's open hangar, the attackers unleash a barrage of fire power. The unit's shield came up, blocking the assault. His pursuers made sharp one hundred and eighty degree turns to retreat right before the unit returned fire.

Too late.

An arc of blue energy shot out and engulfed the enemy. The mid-section of their vehicles disappeared with searing particles floating in the air while the screams were cut off by a second blast of fire. Some of the enemy flailed about, their bodies resembling torches, before falling to the ground. The scout smirked then got out of his transport.

"What the hell were those?" The maintenance tech coming towards him asked.

"Survivors," he replied.

"Fuck me. I'm staying inside."

"Good idea."

The scout walked through the secondary doors that led to the communications room. He needed to report to the leaders.

⸎

Jankowski read the scout's report and slammed his fist down on the glowing table before him. His two colleagues sat still on opposite sides of him waiting for his anger to subside. They had convened to their usual spot in the meeting room and went over all the reports for the day.

"Goddamnit, they got weapons!"

"Of course they do," Omar said. "We expected as much."

"Or did you think they were going to go primitive and have pistols?" Reinhart snorted.

"This is not amusing!" Jankowski snapped.

"Are you done?" Omar asked calmly. When there was no answer, he continued. "We have a new lead on the facility the other team found." He tapped on the map displayed on the table and zoomed in on a live feed.

Well, aren't they bold? Reinhart said silently.

"They're not hiding at all," he said.

"No. I think we should establish some dialogue and let them know our agenda."

"And if they refuse? I hate to be the one beating a dead horse here," Omar said.

"We'll have to think of some kind of failsafe strategy," Jankowski replied.

"Because if the rogue survivors have advanced weapons, that facility has a way bigger arsenal than we have on hand," Reinhart added.

MECCA

Professor Veronica Headland stood with both hands planted firmly on her sleek white desk as she leaned forward, staring out the curtain windows of her office. She let her hair fall over one shoulder while her gaze perused the flow of traffic outside. Her facility was one of the few that remained occupied above ground, her decision, while others went down in the ocean. The new shield system created before the war had held against the onslaught and allowed her to build up a stronghold.

A rainbow sheen glimmered across the dome barrier as muted sunlight cast down creating a stark contrast to the desolate terrain surrounding its perimeter. Within its confines stood a cluster of white buildings, pristine, state of the art. Monorails criss crossed connecting each one as they carried people in uniform to their destinations. None of the inhabitants looked towards the outside.

After ten years, the sky was clearing up. The sun finally penetrated the red clouds and revealed the aftermath of the war. It was not an appealing sight. The charred ground barely held together. Dirty rain had created black mud that clung to any surface it encountered. It was even harder to get off skin and clothes.

Displayed on her desk's surface was a report from one of her own investigators. Scouts were being sent out from every sector, making sure not to step on each other's toes. It was too early in this stage to start a fight without first knowing your opponents. She had read the file numerous times and still could not believe it. On the other hand, she wasn't entirely surprised.

That didn't take long, she thought.

When the rain came and cleared away some of the red clouds allowing inevitable sunshine, she knew a faction of world leaders would come crawling out of the ashes in search of dominance. They saw the potential for a new world do over. She found them to be arrogant and greedy. A request to turn over her systems to the new order was attached to the file and she had hit the decline icon without a thought. Her swift response would bring an even quicker one from the sender.

They've learned nothing!

Her commlink chimed and a second screen appeared on the desk. She hit the connect icon and one of her former colleagues, a scientist now siding with the elite leaders' agenda, came into view.

"Veronica," he said coyly. "Beautiful as ever."

"What do you want?" She asked bluntly.

He frowned then seemed to brush it off.

"How combative. No need for that. I wanted to offer you a chance to join our cause."

"I've already sent a reply telling you no."

"Yes, but you see," he leaned forward, "you are not taking in consideration the perks." His eyes narrowed then. "Or, the consequences if you continue to refuse."

"Is that so?" She straightened her posture. "There are no perks, in my opinion. And, what do you think your group can do to me?"

"We'll tear that little slice of paradise you call a facility apart. You'll have no choice but to turn your communications network and all resources over to the new regime."

"You're forgetting something."

"Oh?" His eyebrows lifted playfully.

"The Litigator."

This time her former colleague's face turned red and his brow furrowed.

"We'll take care of him. Then there will be no issue."

"No one is taking my facility. End of story."

"Don't be naïve. You're nothing but a bunch of lab techs with no combat training. There's no other option for you."

"If you come here, I guarantee you will lose."

"I was trying to be nice, us having worked together back before all this. You've been warned, Veronica."

The screen went blank and Veronica let out a heavy sigh. She looked back out at the sky.

The Litigator.

A being capable of negotiating with the planet itself and causing harm to every living thing while resurfacing Earth. The initial goal was to have him fix the ecosystem but as the war went on, it became clear he had a different idea in mind; the complete eradication of humans. He was out there somewhere contemplating humanity's fate in favor of saving only the planet. His argument was that Earth would thrive much better without humans.

She also had a plan to stop him but hers didn't include murder. He could be reasoned with; she was sure of it. The only problem was time. The new faction of leaders would not wait to move and attack her facility along the way. She needed to get to him first. She needed someone she could trust to make the journey to his last coordinates.

The office doors slid open and her personal assistant, Dr. Alicia Stern came in. The woman was a smaller version of Veronica with similar convictions. She walked over briskly, her white lab coat swaying with the motion. The strike of her military style black boots was muffled by the floor's sound absorbing material. She pushed her black rimmed glasses back on the bridge of her nose and stopped a few feet from Veronica. The woman didn't need them anymore following mandatory vision correction when she was in combat training but wore them for nostalgia sake. Her five-foot six frame was nearly dwarfed by her boss' five eleven height.

"I have gone over the personnel data you asked for," she began.

"And?" Veronica asked as she turned around to face her.

"I think those self-appointed world leaders are in for a rude awakening. What made them think we were all just useless civilians?" She smirked. "I've been known to cut a throat or two back in the day."

"I am well aware." Veronica rested her butt on the edge of her desk. "I need someone to find the Litigator. They plan to kill him."

Alicia scoffed.

"As if they could."

"They must have found a way."

That made her assistant purse her lips.

"If that's the case, then we should hurry."

"But who? Who can I trust with such a task?"

Her fingers gripped the edge, making her knuckles go white.

"Someone unattached but willing to do your bidding," Alicia answered, shrugging.

Veronica gave her an exasperated look and bobbed her head, shrugging herself.

"I'm sure you'll figure it out. Do you want a copy of the data?" Alicia held up the tiny microchip.

"No. Keep it. You're better at assigning those kinds of things."

Her assistant smiled and turned back to leave. When she was in the corridor, the doors slid shut. Veronica walked around to the other side of her desk and stood at the window. Her assistant's words replayed in her head.

Unattached and willing to do my bidding.

Countless residents were beholden to her for letting them stay in the facility. None of them could be categorized as loyal. Everyone had their own agendas. She had nothing to offer in the form of compensation other than what they already acquired.

A thought ran through her head, shocking her. With eyes wide, she mulled it over and felt a bit ill. Over the decades she had birthed and engineered multiple children with her seed and top candidates of compatible DNA. Of the four who were incubated in her private lab all despised her; except one. Xander. He seemed to not dwell on his beginnings, taking advanced courses and using the combat training simulator. A beautiful boy in her eyes, even though she had only seen him on a few occasions.

She thought about how little she interacted with her children and that hurt. The advancement of science to win the war had taken precedence. She wanted to leave a legacy in case she was taken out by her enemies. That meant her children would be in the care of others who were under no obligation to love them. With the war over, she had switched to survival mode. Now she had to deal with delusional power-hungry men. Time to change her views. Tapping the desk to put the screen in sleep mode, she headed out of her office and down the corridor to her private common area.

The area was designated only for personnel under her direct command and those with blood ties. She allowed her children and the workers to have friends visit so at times, the common area was brimming with people. Still, they made up less than one percent of the facility's population.

On a window seat near the far end is where she caught sight of him. With one leg bent on the ledge and the other hanging off, Xander was in a relaxed position at his usual spot. He held a tablet a few inches from his face and she could see he was reading a digital book. His body was long with lean muscle like that of a runner. Jet black hair fell in slight waves across his shoulders. She watched his golden colored eyes rapidly scan the screen, his lips pressed together in earnest.

Two of her other children walked past him. A taller brother and sister with dark brown hair and bulkier frames. The brother, Caleb, was the one closest to him carrying a drink. Without warning, the drink was tossed on Xander, its contents landing on his bodysuit and streaking the window. To her surprise, he merely sat up, wiped the excess from microscales of the black bodysuit and tablet before leaning back against the ledge. The two siblings snorted and continued walking. Her daughter, Christine, caught her stare and frowned, tugging Caleb. They both gave her a nasty look as they left the area.

They won't forgive me.

Her mind made up, Veronica turned and went back to her office. There was so much she needed to prepare before sending him on such a dangerous mission. Only her assistant would know the details of the mission. He had to make it back alive, no matter what. She felt the need to fix their relationship.

⌁

After two days of haggling with Alicia about logistics and threat assessments, Veronica was finally satisfied with the plan. She plopped down in her office chair and exhaled loudly, letting her head fall back. She stayed like that for a while before sitting up straight and tapping the commlink icon on her desk.

A woman appeared on the screen.

"Good afternoon, Professor Headland. What can I do for you?"

"Send Xander to my office. Please make sure he is not followed."

"Will he not need an escort?" Her expression became dubious.

Her children were not permitted to roam her area without armed guards. There had been many incidents where they attacked her unprovoked. That said, the one she was requesting never did such a thing. He was always quiet, never moving from where he stood like a soldier at ease.

"No. Send him alone. You will tell no one, understand?"

"Of course, Professor."

"Thank you."

She disconnected the feed and settled back in her chair to wait. There was a knock on the door before it slid open and her son walked in. He was indeed beautiful. She nearly caught her breath at the sight of him. The same features as his father, tall and slender, with her face. A few feet from the desk, he stopped, appearing uncomfortable.

"Please, sit. I'm not going to hurt you."

"I know. I'm just nervous." His voice was a soft alto that made her heart skip.

"Why?"

"You never really talk to me, or the others. I'm never sure how to react."

Veronica gave him a pained smile.

"And, I regret that. I want to get to know you better."

"But right now, you need me to do something for you." He said it nonchalantly.

She motioned for him to come closer and reached over her desk to remove his arms from behind his back then grabbed both his hands.

"Please know, I do not want to do this. I would rather have one of the combat soldiers do it. But…"

"You can't trust them."

Veronica let go of his hands and stood, walking around the desk to his side. She cupped his face in her hands.

"I will tell you why this task is important." Veronica let go and sat on the edge of her desk. "The Litigator is willing to manipulate the planet for its survival at our expense. Any more global seismic shifts would be catastrophic since we have barely recovered. I want to negotiate with him to come up with a better solution. I may not get the chance if a faction of world leaders have their way." Her fingers came up to form quotation marks as she said it.

"World leaders?" He asked. "According to who?"

"Themselves. They want to dominate the world. Restore order. And, kill the Litigator."

"But, why? He can just as easily fix parts of the planet."

"Because like me, they don't trust many people, least of all aliens."

"You want me to find the Litigator. How am I supposed to convince him?"

"However you see fit. Come."

Veronica slid off the desk and walked towards the door. She stopped and waited for him to follow. Together they walked into the corridor and down to the end where a lift sat opened for them. Once inside, she swiped her hand across the control panel, the doors closed and it shot down into the depths of the facility. It jerked to a stop moments later and opened to a large hangar.

Various transport units were scattered around. Hovercrafts, road vehicles, and aerial fighters. Her son looked around in awe.

They came to a white and grey, road vehicle nearly six feet in height with a blue racer stripe. She used a remote to open the passenger door. Inside was everything needed to survive a long journey. Food packs filled the storage bins along with plenty of electrolyte water. The side panel in the back seat folded out to reveal a personal medical unit.

"Wow," Xander exclaimed.

"It has full autopilot, so you don't have to manually drive if you don't want to." He nodded while continuing his inspection of the vehicle. She pulled him away and made him face her. "Listen to me." His expression turned to fear. She sighed and placed her hands on his cheeks. "You must come back. Do you understand? I need you to get home safe."

They locked eyes. He finally relaxed, leaning into her. She hugged him tight.

"Promise me."

"I promise," he whispered.

She let him go and stepped back.

"Now hurry. I want you far away from here before those idiots show up. The Litigator's last known coordinates are programmed in the navigation system."

He climbed in the driver's seat and pushed the start button. The doors came down and sealed him in. The dash lit up and all the systems booted up along with the AI.

"System ready. Proceeding with drive sequence."

The AI was female, her voice soothing. Xander began

to familiarize himself with the controls as the hangar doors opened to the outside. The barrier was shut down in the area allowing only enough room for the vehicle to clear. As it shot forth towards the wastelands, leaving the safety of the facility, Veronica's knees buckled. She slid to the floor sobbing.

Alicia came up behind her and laid a hand on her shoulder.

"He understood perfectly."

"I know," Veronica sobbed. "That's why it hurts."

The hangar closed with the barrier back in place.

Her son was on his own now.

Dried clumps of earth the size of boulders loosened themselves from the sides of a deep crevice and tumbled down in what used to be part of the ocean. On the edge of the cliff, a large section that appeared to be part of it jutted out over the barren landscape. Beneath the caked mud and petrified roots sat Facility three. The only visible part of it was the landing platform on the roof. Sections of white metal had been exposed by the elements over the years.

Inside, the people kept busy. Most were scientists while the rest were Bi-Genetics, some with high level talents who kept themselves contained. The once bright main corridors now emitted low yellow light to conserve energy. Blocked off bays damaged from the battle sat in darkness. Scientists had long ditched their lab coats in favor of scrubs or bodysuits since they were easier to reproduce and clean. Facility Three's current population was just above four thousand. Enough to make sure the place ran efficiently without hiccups.

Above the main hub, Professor Bartley sat in a swivel chair before the viewing pane of his private quarters watching the slow moving activities throughout the facility. His dark wavy hair was freshly trimmed to above his shoulders and he was clean shaven. Beside him, multiple holoscreens displayed each section, including the outside.

His eyes narrowed.

News of the new faction had traveled to him and at first, he felt nothing, citing the inevitable. Now, it angered him. After all that had transpired, humans were still selfish and greedy for power. He had viewed each video report noting the landscape crawling with men in white hazmat suits collecting specimens. The rear hangar had only been opened four times in the last ten years out of necessity. He was not going to send out scouts when he had Bi-Genetics with telepathy, third eye sight, and clairvoyance.

Motion on one of the screens caught his eye and he turned to its attention. Vasence was waving to him from the corridor outside his lab. He then walked through the open disabled entrance. There was no reason to keep the doors sealed anymore. Bartley switched to the lab's feed and Vasence was on the videochat.

"What can I do for you, Professor Vasence?"

"It's not me," he replied followed by a long sigh. "Lillian the Great wants to have a word with you. And since, she currently occupies my lab..." He didn't finish the sentence, making a bowing gesture and stepped to the side.

In his place stood Dr. Lillian Shriever looking better than when she first arrived during the war. Her hair was uncharacteristically pulled back in a tight ponytail showing the scar running the length of her face on one side. Despite the consensus for scrubs, she had opted to keep wearing her lab coat over them.

During the battle, she and a small crew stayed behind to ensure every primer still in incubation and all personnel were evacuated before the lab was completely destroyed. Even though she didn't send out a distress signal, Vasence had been monitoring the Primer Facility and made the last moment decision to save them via forced teleport. Making them the only survivors left standing afterwards

"Professor Bartley," she began in haste. "I know I don't have to tell you that we need to activate the defense systems. If the old world leaders were willing to let most of the human race die, there's no telling what they are capable of now."

Bartley exhaled through his nose, pursing his lips. He understood her advice, just not the timing of it. Firing up weapons and reestablishing security protocols did not seem necessary at this juncture.

"I agree, they are a danger. Nevertheless, we are safe for now. If need be, the system can be brought back online within hours."

"What if we don't have hours?" She snapped. "You don't even know if they're still operational. The last time they worked was during the war."

"She has a point," Vasence interjected, leaning into the frame of the screen.

"They are not that fast, or savvy for that matter, to cause a panic. We can wait and see what they do. If it looks like an issue, I will give the order."

"Professor!" Dr. Shriever yelled. "Don't play a dangerous game. With the collapse of civilization…"

Bartley leaned forward, his eyes reflected on the screen changed color from blue to yellow, the lines a thick dark brown. Her face went pale and she stepped back from the table the screen hovered over. Vasence took a deep breath and stepped back in sight.

"Don't get worked up over this," Vasence suggested. "She is right, the new faction is a threat. But I told her to respect your judgement on this."

Bartley sat back, his eyes returned to normal, and contemplated the issue. What infuriated him the most was that her assessment of the weapons system might be dead on.

For all he knew, the power cells had either stalled or drained. He read the message from Veronica regarding the dispatch of her son to negotiate with the Litigator. It was a foolish gamble, in his opinion. There was no telling what that creature had going on in his head. Yet, he couldn't fault her for trying. His emergency commlink lit up and one of the guards at the main entrance came into view.

"What is it?" He demanded. "What's happening?"

"Umm," the young guard began, "we have incoming."

"Say what?"

"Survivors, sir. They are seeking refuge."

"How many?"

The view change to a wide screen and he saw a large number of people huddled together at the edge of the cliff. From their demeanor and clothing, he could tell; they were broken. He counted a little over a hundred.

"Let them in. Make sure they go through the quarantine chambers on entry."

"Yes sir." The guard's feed ended.

Barley tapped the allcom for the facility.

"All personnel, prepare for incoming. Medical units start recovery sequence. Hospitality please meet with the guards at the post quarantine exits."

Vasence came back onscreen.

"Are you insane?" He cried out. "There could be spies in their midst."

"All the more reason, don't you think?"

A sinister thought conveyed on Vasence's face as he leaned back from the screen.

"If you're going to go that far, at least let me have

them for research," he muttered.

Bartley glared at him.

"I'm not killing anyone." Then he seemed to contemplate what a spy might be capable of. "Yet."

The scout watched from five kilometers away as the top front section of Facility Three rose up with a loud whine to open the main entrance hangar. Debris, not disturbed for a decade and fused together, cracked, and fell off in chunks. Guards ushered in the large crowd with haste to avoid the fallout while checking their surroundings as they moved.

At the entry, a handheld scanner was waved over each individual before they advanced further. There weren't any weapons and they didn't need any. He chided himself. Most facilities had Bi-Genetics with talent deadlier than any manmade weapon. But he was certain there wasn't that many inside. And now he knew a way to infiltrate the facilities.

Bless their bleeding stupid hearts.

PURSUERS

Commander Fravral stared in awe at the swirls of orange, pink, and red that filled the sky as the wind picked up, carrying the clouds farther out. He was amazed that the red mist spreading death had took so long to dissipate. His tattered cloak swayed with the breeze, giving a glimpse of his dark grey battle suit still intact. And he needed it. In the short period of time since the battle, he witnessed the decline of human civilization. There was a desperate sense of survival with disregard for their fellow man.

In the secondary hatch of the transport his Cybok kept shelter. The being rarely came out and when he did, it was to crush whatever enemy the two had encountered. Fravral found the Cybok's assistance against the humans unnecessary. He understood why. The Cybok was trained for combat. With the battle over, the being relished in any kind of fight.

When his ship crashed on Earth after colliding with another engulfed in flames, he cursed his luck. He could still see the other Cybok move to shield him as it made impact. The blast killed him instantly, eighty percent of his body disintegrated, while it blocked the rest from getting to Fravral and the other Cybok.

Glancing back at the hatch, he wondered if his Cybok was feeling remorse or sorrow. There was a strange expression on his face when they emerged from the wreckage. It had never occurred to him if the two spent any time together when not on duty.

That's a failure on my part.

Chaos was all around them and the red mist had already saturated the area. Relenting to his situation, he stayed put. Gragor had sacrificed so much for the humans' sake. Curious as to the reason, he decided to try to understand them. In the meantime, he needed to get his instruments working so he could locate the missing commander. Every day he would remove the remote fob from the main console and venture out of the zone for a signal. Whenever he got one, they would move towards it before losing the signal. In this new sector there was nothing so far. The two Relliants hunkered down for the long haul.

Now Fravral contemplated giving up the mission. Finding Gragor would be like searching for a black speck on a sandy seashore. He was almost certain the commander would have survived untouched. Inhaling deep, he exhaled slowly before going back to his dilapidated ship. With the wind picking up, he could venture out and scout the area for hostiles. The ship may be a wreck, but it was still operational which attracted those humans looking to gain an edge in the aftermath.

He grabbed one of the handguns confiscated during the last brawl and headed out towards the horizon. The Cybok would come out at the first hint of trouble so he was comfortable leaving. Dark dust swirled around his ankles as he went off. For two hours he searched then headed back.

As he neared his small patch of territory, he spotted two fairly small humans coming out of the ship. There were a few supplies in their hands. Both stopped abruptly upon seeing him and stood still.

Fravral's eyes widened in disbelief right as the transport hatch opened. The Cybok emerged like a creature coming out of the abyss. The girl dropped what was in her arms and backed away. The boy on the other hand, gripped what was in his hand and moved slowly to the girl's side. Fravral watched in horror as the boy pocketed the locator fob...and ran. The girl followed.

"Get back here!" Fravral yelled.

He chased after them. The Cybok was fully out of the hatch and powering up his arm cannons to thirty percent power. To their surprise, the two humans flash stepped off into the distance. The Cybok's blast missed them. Fravral cursed inwardly. He had never mastered that technique and the Cybok did not have the capability to move that fast. Turning back to the Cybok, he called out to him.

"Can you track their scent?" The Cybok's eyes glowed as he glared at him and simply nodded. "Good. I'm going to seal the ship and we're going after those brats." He smirked, hearing himself use the human term. It definitely fit, in his opinion.

The Cybok's arm cannons reverted back to normal and he climbed back into the hatch. Fravral sighed and went into the ship. He brought up the main system grid and tapped on the shield icon. As he cleared its proximity, the barrier expanded out around the ship. Satisfied, he went to the transport's cockpit and settled in. He fired up the engines and waited until the transport was a good twenty feet off the ground before hitting the thrusters. Even with the two humans flash stepping across the plains, he was certain he could catch up to them.

"Let's hunt some humans," he said more to himself.

Black mud kicked up from the heels of the two runners' boots as they sprinted across the barren wastelands of what was left of the United States of America. Nothing could be seen for miles except a few mounds of clumped rock randomly scattered.

The young man leading them looked up at the sky without slowing his pace. His dark hair was cut short, the edges uneven from the makeshift knife he had used on it. There was caked dirt on his waterproof tunic and his utility cargo shorts were filthy. Eyes the color of blue steel peered at the gathering clouds.

More rain.

Behind him, his younger sister kept in step, her stride shorter so she didn't overtake him. She was a little taller than him with brown hair. Her eyes were a shade darker. She too glanced up. Wearing the same outfit, equally appearing broken down from wear and tear, she seemed unfazed.

Both were thinking the same thing. Shelter. They had taken it every which way they could. Ship wrecks, collapsed hills, caverns created by fallen mountain boulders, and the rare abandoned bunker left open or its seal broken. As luck would have it, they never went more than twenty miles without finding something. From their calculations, there would be something in another six miles which meant they might get caught in the dirty rain for at least a mile before finding one.

Not speaking conserved their energy while running. And they needed all they could after using the flash step technique multiple times earlier to get away from that crazed looking soldier and the giant that was with him.

At the start of their journey, they had carried a lot of supplies in backpacks. When it became too much of a burden, slowing them down, they agreed to drop most of their load. With less weight, they were able to run faster, covering more miles in a day than before. Of course, there were times when they needed certain things and had to resort to stealing or rummaging through wreckage.

Times were hard. The young man didn't understand why the man was so upset. He was sure there had been others who stumbled upon the ship and found something useful. At the same time, he knew what his sister and he were doing was wrong. What disturbed him the most was the giant who came out of the other ship. A mass of black tendrils whipping in the wind with glowing blue eyes that pierced through his very soul. Thinking back, he realized it must have been the thing in his pocket. Too late now.

They're gonna' chase us.

Dark water began to spit out of the sky right as the young man spotted a crumbled structure up ahead. The spattering left dark splotches on his face. He pressed his lips tight together so not to get any in his mouth while he pulled the attached face shield on his shirt up to his nose. His sister did the same. They made a last-minute dash to the structure, arriving in time before the drizzle became a downpour.

As they entered the place, they took in their surroundings. It always amazed them how some of the buildings survived the blasts and the red mist of death. This building appeared to have been part of a commercial property. The rest of it was crumbled debris alongside it. The siblings pulled their face shields down and started inspection.

"Hey, Seth," she said while running a hand along the walls. "Look at this. Reinforced construction. They must have built this during the preparations era."

He walked slowly into the dark space, turning his head up to make sure nothing was lurking above them.

"That's probably why it's the only thing left. Whatever

was in here must have been important," she continued.

He heard his sister make a sharp intake of breath and turned towards her.

"Look!" She pointed to a thick metal door slightly cracked open. Its entry scanner was damaged, dangling from its casing. Her eyes pulsed silver. "Should we?" She asked in sinister tone.

"Sure," he said.

His eyes grew brighter as his vision adjusted to accommodate the darkness that enveloped them going in. Stairs leading down into an abyss greeted them. They moved steadily, close together, descending the narrow pathway. At the bottom, they came into a large room with metal shelves and cabinets that closed flat into the walls. Some were sitting open empty or their contents hanging out.

They stopped near the center. A dozen dead bodies lay strewn around the room. Their level of decomposition put them at over two years dead. Five of them wore lab technician jumpsuits while the rest wore peculiar handcrafted outfits and face paint. The young man knelt by the one closest to him and saw the cybernetic arm bent underneath.

"Modified soldiers gone rogue," his sister whispered. "I hate seeing that."

"Yeah."

He stood back up and glanced around, reading the labels along the walls. Consumable provisions, tech and edible. The place had been hit hard. Most of the supplies were still intact though. A short-lived fight. That made him wonder what caused them to leave in a hurry in the middle of a raid despite losing only a few men.

"Want to wait out the storm upstairs?" She asked.

Seth nodded, stepping over a few of the bodies to get to one of the shelves on the far end. There were vacuum sealed packets with full meal replacement capsules combined with vitamins. Next to those were new generation MREs that could be consumed dry or mixed with water. Each individual silver wrapped bag was in the form of a small cake two inches in diameter.

"Found something useful," his sister called out.

He turned around and saw her wagging a small knapsack. It was obviously designed for the provisions. Light weight mesh outer layer, and the size of two footballs flattened side by side. These were way better than the bulky things they had back then. These, they could deal with and not have any issues. She began to model its functionality. It could be worn in the front or back of the body. Its straps were made to crisscross for stability.

"Lucky!" She squealed excitedly. "Let's load them up."

On the tech side, he used his foot to shove one of the bodies out of the way and opened a wall unit labeled filters. There were new credit card sized water treatment filters along with a compact device that accompanied them. He pulled the heavier older version out of one of his cargo pants pocket and tossed it on the floor. It felt like a brick had been removed from one side of his body.

He turned back to her and called out, "Erin."

She looked over her shoulder at him, her shopping halted.

"Dinner?" He glanced at the shelf of MREs.

"Do they have mash potatoes and gravy?"

He sighed and gave her an irritated expression. She grinned and stuck her tongue out of the side of her lips. It was one of the few food dishes she confessed to liking when she was little. The real stuff though. He figured they probably wouldn't see real food again for a long time.

As the two siblings arranged the items for packing, they both got a nudge inside their heads. Seth looked over at his sister then stood. He scanned the area and found nothing as always. It had been happening at random times for the past two years. He had an idea what it was and it made him sad. His sister would skirt the topic whenever it occurred. They had grown up without parents, raised by government employees whose jobs were to make sure they didn't have access to the outside world.

Not long after the facility collapsed, setting them free, they got the first nudge. Their mother was searching for them. He cut the connection and went back to packing. Even though he wanted to be reunited, he also knew it was too dangerous. Granted, for all he knew, their mother was probably one hell of a soldier. There were rumors that she was one of the first aliens they removed from a crash wreckage. He also knew of the horrible things the human scientists had done to her.

"What do you think she's like?" Erin asked.

He turned to her, shocked that she was broaching the subject.

"Maybe she's pretty like me," she continued.

He smiled, then nodded.

⌒

The rain was too much for Fravral so he found a structure in the opposite direction of where the two humans went. He'd been in other sectors where it rained but it was nothing like this. The dark water etched light scratches into the metal alloy of the ship. Once underneath the shelter he did a quick scan and found it to be a large piece of wreckage from one of the Relliance battle ships. He wondered where the rest of it was and if it may be part of his. It had broken apart long before entering Earth's atmosphere.

He opened the view shield and watched the rainfall from a safe position. The way it coated everything, turning the ground into that disgusting black mud almost made him miss Rellia.

Almost.

The overcrowded walkways and massive housing structures jammed packed with people were less to be desired. When he was chosen to be part of the Command Fleet, he rejoiced at having a place to move around in. Even better as he rose in ranks, getting his own quarters.

Now, here he was alone with a Cybok on a nearly destroyed planet surrounded by vast plains of nothingness. Relaxing in the cockpit, he closed his eyes and let the sounds of the rain pelting the shelter lull him to sleep.

The silence is what startled Fravral awake. He sat up and focused on the view outside. The rain was gone, replaced by the strange colors of sunlight struggling through the clouds. Tapping the commlink for the attached transport, he called out to the Cybok.

"You awake in there? We're moving out."

He didn't wait for a reply. There was no need. He fired up the transport system and made sure the coordinates were still the same.

"Little thieves! I'll catch up to you soon. Just wait."

A MOTHER'S INTUITION

Grannalt reared back from the psychic backlash as his thoughts were blocked off like a door slamming in his face. He had sent out tendrils of his consciousness out to his children and was only able to find two of them. The other three he assumed must have died unless they had intentionally severed the connection. Each time he reached out to the two he was able to get a better grasp on their location. What he felt this time before being denied was fear.

"He's worried about my safety," Grannalt mused.

He wrapped the fur lined coat around him and sat back against the wall inside an abandoned installation he had stumbled across. A heat flare glowed on the floor with a few packs of rations surrounding it. They had gotten too cold to come out of the sealed bags so he was warning them up, and himself.

Certain parts of the region had different climates, making travel difficult depending on how much supplies one needed to haul. Judging by the moisture in the air, and what he had encountered weather wise so far, he could tell the weather about fifty miles out was going to be balmy. He couldn't wait to ditch the heavier stuff.

My children are being chased.

That fact alone made him anxious enough to get closer so he could protect them. But why? He couldn't figure out what caused the Relliant Commander with his Cybok in tow, go after his children.

Late in the morning he headed back out. The trail was lukewarm but Grannalt soldiered on. He took stock of the wastelands' condition as he traveled. Some of the territories had small villages which he steered clear of. Traditional currency was obsolete, replaced with bartering. He could only imagine what the trade market entailed, and he didn't like any of the options.

Wearing a battered cloak, its hem raggedy from years of abuse, and his original battle suit found in a storage bin at the now crumbled heap that used to be the cannon base, Grannalt resembled a sand merchant. His face and head were wrapped in the loose fabric of the hood and secured with extra strips of similar material. Only his eyes were visible. Underneath the cloak was a phaser and the housing mechanism for a laser blade. So far, he had used them both twice. Each time to defend himself against crazed humans who seemed to have lost their humanity.

As he crossed into a new terrain, the weather changed abruptly. No more dry, dusty wind, the air was calm and the pinkish orange sky clear. He undid a few of the cloth strips around his neck to let the hood fall back, exposing his jet-black hair. Most of it was tucked under the cloak due to how long it had gotten over the past year. To his dismay, he spotted a dark shimmer in the distance. A village. From the swirl of dust surrounding it, he could tell what kind of people inhabited there.

The area was wide open so no matter where we went, he would be seen. He watched the inevitable as part of the dust cloud changed direction and began to move towards him. A single vehicle raced across the caked mud surface, sending chunks of it flying behind. Grannalt counted five men in the modified SUV, its top removed and replaced with a roll bar across the middle. There were no weapons mounted on it which Grannalt was relieved for. The vehicle swerved in a sharp arc and stopped fifty yards from him.

The driver and two from the back jumped out, proud smiles on their faces.

"Well, lookit here," the driver drawled. "Got us a traveler."

"Where ya' headed?" One of the men from the back asked, circling behind Grannalt.

"Just passing through," Grannalt replied softly.

The other man was mere inches from him in a heartbeat, forcing Grannalt to step back closer the other one. He was trapped in the triangle formation they created around him.

"I know those eyes," the man sneered. "You're one of them aliens that crash landed."

That made the other two still in the vehicle perk up and jump out to join their comrades.

"Looks pretty to me," the front passenger laughed.

"Huh," the driver smirked. "Been a while since I got to desecrate a Biode for fun."

He reached out to touch Grannalt's hair. His counterparts gave him a weird look for getting the two things mixed up then shrugged.

"I say we have a bit of fun," the one behind Grannalt added. "Take him back so the rest can have a turn."

Before the driver's hand brushed the top of his head, Grannalt grabbed it and twisted down, bending with it. He heard the bone snap. The driver cried out in pain and with his other hand, punched Grannalt in the side of his face. The man behind Grannalt looped his arms under his and pulled Grannalt back into a body lock.

One of the other men from the back, came up and punched Grannalt in the stomach. All the air left his body and he coughed up blood. Shocked by the power of the assault, Grannalt looked up at the man's hand and saw a mesh metal glove.

You piece of shit! Grannalt cursed him.

The driver stood up and hit him again before reaching under the cloak to grab one of his legs.

"Now we're gonna' make it hurt worse than we planned, you fucking alien."

The one holding him went down on his knees to force Grannalt to the ground. Grannalt felt the other men grab onto the bodysuit, searching for sections of looseness. One of them took hold of his hair, the strands getting tangled between his fingers while he pulled out a blade, ready to cut through the suit.

Grannalt suddenly had a flash back to a couple of years after he was captured. When the guards kept watched while their counterparts raped him repeatedly for days until the head scientist found out and put him in isolation. That didn't stop that sort of thing from happening again and again over the decades.

Full of rage, Grannalt's fighting instinct returned once again and he brought his head back into the man's behind him. At first, the man simply faltered as his head snapped back, his gripped still firm. When it came upright, Grannalt feeling his anger, he headbutted him again, this time hard enough that he heard a cracking sound. The man's grip ceased, his body falling to the ground. In the moment of surprise, he got a leg loose and kicked the man on his left in the neck.

The driver rushed him, pinning a knee into Grannalt's chest while raising his fist to deliver a blow. His comrade to his right was also ready with his mesh gloved fist. Grannalt dug along the side of bodysuit with his fingers and closed them around the laser blade hilt. Right as both men's fist came down mere inches from his face, he swung out wide, pushing the activation button. The white hot laser shot out, slicing through both forearms and nicking the driver's face right across the left eye.

Both men shouted in despair, falling back from Grannalt. He got on his feet and faced the remaining two who brandished weapons. One had a hunting knife in each hand, the other, a small cylinder that when pushed down extended into a six foot rod. The man demonstrated his skills by spinning the rod around his waist and into the air before pointing it towards him in a crouched stance.

Grannalt tilted his head in confusion. Is that it? After witnessing the relentless brutality of Lieutenant Sspark's attacks, this man was subpar. Drowning out the screaming from the two men still writhing on the ground in pain, bleeding out, he went into his own fight stance and dug his heels in the dirt. The two men advanced, letting out primal yells. Grannalt brought the laser blade in position at a one-hundred-and-twenty-degree angle and flash stepped towards them. At the last moment, he pressed the density button on the module as he swung multiple times, coming out from between them.

He stopped. His feet dragged through the dirt, leaving skid marks and turned around. The two men also stopped a few feet apart from each other with looks of shock on their faces. Deep, bloody cuts covered the front and sides of their bodies. They managed to glance at themselves then fall unconscious onto the ground.

The driver rolled onto his back and glared at him with his one good eye.

"We're gonna kill you! Our buds are going to realize we ain't back and come for us. You got nowhere to run."

Grannalt stared down at him with enough malice to make the man flinch.

He deactivated the laser blade and reattached it to his bodysuit.

"Oh, I'll be long gone," Grannalt said. He went over to the vehicle and climbed into the driver seat. "I'm going to borrow this."

He hit the ignition and put the vehicle in gear. Giving the five men one last look, he gunned the accelerator and sped off. His tangled hair whipped into his face and he used one hand to push it back down in the cloak. A smile crept up. He enjoyed that fight, albeit short lived. Before he was a captive, he was a soldier. Even the battle that scorched this planet fueled his juices, allowing him to exact revenge on a few humans along with the Relliants. Shaking his head to rid of those thoughts, he focused on his current agenda.

I'm coming, my children.

⌣

Kevin was awakened by weight on his chest. Not heavy but enough to make him aware that something was atop him. When tiny fingers dug into his shirt, he knew it was the little one again. His son, born from Terence without his consent or knowledge. He knew it was not the child's fault yet, Kevin felt hostility. The boy only wanted to be near him. Kevin was not ready for that.

"Get off," he commanded. He felt hesitation and sadness. That made him feel guiltier, but he continued. "Now."

He opened his eyes and found himself staring into the little boy's. Tears started to well up and his son hung his head. Kevin let out a loud sigh. He grabbed the boy under the armpits and moved him aside onto the bed. At ten years old, he was quite small for his age. His brown hair and violet eyes were the perfect combination of his parents.

When Kevin came out of his coma, five years had passed. His anger was palpable. Even his children chastised him for his reaction. He had slammed an already weakened Terence into the wall, his face contorted in rage as he demanded an explanation. For a year, he stewed, avoiding the child at all costs. Terence tried to plead with him and instead, Kevin forced himself on her, claiming that was what she wanted, right? Now, with two children by Terence, he hated himself for doing it.

"Why are you in here?" He asked his son. The boy's lips quivered. "I asked you a question. There's no reason for you to cry!" His son let out a wail and he stood from the bed. "Damn it!"

Terence came into the room, her face stricken with despair. She zeroed in on their son and went towards him. Kevin stopped her.

"Are you going to coddle him every time he can't handle something?" He watched Terence's expression crumble and it angered him. Her body was in a state of flux, not as powerful as it once was. "How did he get in here, anyway?"

"I'm sorry," Terence whispered.

Shame consumed him but he wouldn't back down. Stepping to the side, he let Terence scoop up their son and carry him out. He caught sight of the three-year-old coming out of hiding from the corner of the doorway and follow them down the hall.

"Fuck!"

Kevin turned around and snatched his commlink wristband off the side table. As he slapped it on while heading out himself, he saw Otto standing in his way.

"Dad," he said. "I swear, if you ever hurt them, I will fight you. I won't win, but you'll know how we all feel about the way you treat them and Terence."

Kevin frowned.

He forced himself not to look hurt by it and gave Otto a smirk.

"Oh? You're going to come at me?"

"I'm not joking, dad."

With that, Otto turned away and left the corridor, leaving Kevin dumbstruck. This wasn't how it was supposed to be.

Terence made it back to her private quarters and set her son down on his bed positioned right next to hers. He rarely slept in it, opting to sleep with her and his younger brother. He gave her a sorrowful look and she smile, patting her bed. He crawled over, careful to avoid the gap, and curled up in her lap. The three-year-old did the same, making her thighs hurt. She didn't care about that; she could endure their weight. Tears streamed down her cheeks.

She understood Kevin's rage. The consequences of her actions were not lost. Still, he had no right to take it out on their children. They were babies without sin. If it ever became clear that he would harm them, she was ready to put him down with everything she had.

Her chamber door opened, surprising her. West, her second in command, came into the room.

"I shouldn't have to tell you that he is dangerous and needs to leave."

"He's angry," she started to explain.

"No excuse. I will not tolerate it much longer. It's bringing down moral."

Terence glanced over at him and saw for the first time how rundown he was. His hair was combed back yet there were signs of tangled strands. The dark circle under his eyes made him look even more sinister. In place of his uniform, he wore a tight-fitting black shirt and khaki cargo pants with black combat boots. His hands were behind his back as he stood At Ease.

Terror Operative.

Terence winced at the term. The last thing she wanted was for the people inside Metropolis reverting to their old ways when under the command of the senior General Hoskins. She slowly sat up, letting the boys slide off on each side of her with ease and moved to the edge of the bed. He backed away a few steps not wanting her to touch him.

"We will endure. Please, let me handle this. I promise. Things will get better."

"Is that so?" He asked vehemently. "Are you back at full strength?" When she didn't answer right away, he stepped back into the corridor. "Right. Then you can do nothing."

He pivoted away from her and marched down the walkway as her chamber door shut.

"Momma." The three-year-old came behind her and wrapped his arms around her right bicep. "It's okay. We still love you and Daddy."

Terence nearly choked as she turned to look down at him. His grey eyes mirrored the smile on his cherub face. That did it. Kevin would not bully them any longer. Her children were top priority.

Kevin stood around the corner at the end of the hall. He waited for West to pass him before speaking.

"You'll know when I become dangerous."

West stopped and glanced back at him.

"Oh, I already know you are. The question is when to put you down like the animal you've become."

Kevin's eyes glowed as he drew up energy then remembered he was in a contained environment. West smirked at his realization.

"If you hurt them, it will be the last day for you here. I suggest you go on your own."

"I would never hurt my kids!"

"Oh? Do you not verbally and psychologically abuse them and their mother?"

Before Kevin could answer, West strode off. He caught sight of the man's uniform as well and hissed in anguish. What could have possessed the commander to start reverting into a Terror? Instead of going for a walk in the manufactured garden, he waited for West to go in the first lift then followed him up in the next one.

He entered the main hub of Metropolis and into a flurry of activity. The holoscreens were displaying images from all over. Each console was manned with technicians go over data. West stopped walking and turned to him.

"Why have you come up here?"

"Because you're acting like a Terror operative ready to go to war."

West's lips went thin. His eyes glowed a pale lavender from still having some of the Organic's modifications

"If it comes to that, so be it."

"If it…what the hell is going on? What have you been keeping from us? From Terence?"

"Terence knows the situation."

"Then I don't!" Kevin went to stand a few feet from him. "You're going to enlighten me?"

West averted his attention to the holoscreens above.

"There is a faction of former elites calling them-selves the New World Order."

Kevin sputtered, his eyes wide in amusement.

"Say again? You're joking." West gave him a nasty stare. "You can't possibly take this seriously."

The middle screen changed to show a white transport with land to air cannons surrounded by troops in white uniforms with New Oder insignias. They plowed through a hostile territory firing upon them. The fight was over in minutes concluded by a white flag emblazoned with the new order insignia. Kevin balked at the scene.

"Those sons of bitches," he whispered.

"Their plan is to take out the Litigator so he doesn't mess things up, leaving an easy open to snatch up the territories and claim a new society."

"Take out," Kevin began. "The Litigator?" He tilted his head and blinked a few times.

"That's their plan along with hostile takeover of the facilities to establish a communication network."

Then it hit him. Metropolis was a giant property that was equivalent to four facilities in one. If the new order could get their hands on it, they were golden. Of course, that was never going to happen under West or Terence's watch. Even so, with the amount of fire power he witnessed, a fight was imminent.

"How big a risk we talking?"

"They have locations full of weapons. They have spread far enough that they can tap any one of them as needed. By the time they get to our location, they will have a full army."

"Mother fucker." Kevin's eyes burned. "And Terence knows all of this?"

"As she should. It's her damn facility. I can't keep something like this from her."

Anger came over Kevin. For Terence to go through this alone without bringing him in on it spoke to her lack of trust. He understood his actions were not ideal but she should know he would always back her in a fight. Reeling from the information and what felt like betrayal, he headed back to the lift. That walk in the garden was sounding like the right thing to do.

His feelings were irrational, he knew that, yet he still left the garden after three hours of solitude ready to tear something apart. Kevin took a few deep breaths as he neared Terence's personal chamber. The door was open and he could hear her laughing followed by soft giggles from their children.

Stay calm, stay calm, stay calm!

The moment he stepped into the room it went silent. All three looked over at him with stunned faces. His anger sparked.

Breath.

"I heard something quite interesting from your commander." Terence bit her lower lip as she stared at him. "You want to guess what it was?"

"He told you."

"You!" Kevin yelled, "Should have told me!"

She flinched and the little ones clung to her.

"I…we…were handling it," she said softly.

"Why? Why didn't you tell me? Don't you trust me?"

Terence stood and walked towards the door.

"It's not about trust. This is the facility I built. It's my duty to protect it."

"And I can't?"

Terence's facial expression turned dark which angered Kevin more. From behind him in the hall he heard his middle son.

"What's going on? Dad?"

"Why are you being as asshole about this? You're not obligated to stay here and defend Metropolis." Terence's hands balled up at her sides. "I don't need you to save me!"

Kevin felt his body grow cold and energy stirred around him. Before he could stop it, his eyes glowing a pale green, wind gathered in the small space and he pushed. Terence's eyes widened as their ten-year-old ran in front of her.

"Don't hurt Momma!"

Too late.

Kevin watch in horror as the blast of air hit his son, slamming him into the wall next to the bed as Terence was thrown back onto it. The energy died along with Kevin's internal struggle.

His shoulders slumped and he stepped forward, one hand reaching out.

"Stay away from him!" His middle son yelled as he pushed his way into the chamber. "What is wrong with you? What have you done?"

Terence forced herself up and went to her son lying unconscious on the floor. The three-year-old started screaming, tears streaming down his rapidly redden face. Kevin backed out of the room, grief stricken.

"You need to leave." West was at the end of the hall flanked by two operatives. They were ready to play. "I warned you."

"So did I," came Otto's voice.

Kevin turned around and was struck in the face. He saw stars from the pain then darkness.

My son knocked me out.

Kevin sat up wincing at the throb above his eyes. He took a look around and found himself in the infirmary. A few feet from the edge of his bed was West. A knapsack sat at his feet and the operative next to him had a set of clothes folded neatly in his arms.

"Want to help the cause so badly? Go find the Litigator before those jackasses do."

The operative set the clothes on the bed. Kevin picked up the first piece. A microtech fiber bodysuit with reinforced mesh.

"The weather is sporadic at best. This will protect you

from the elements. And a knife fight if you find yourself in one of those."

Kevin dropped the bodysuit and hung his head.

"How is my son?"

In a flash, West was on him, a handful of his shirt in the man's grip.

"You don't get to ask that question." His voice was low and seething. "Get your gear, go up the main level and leave. An operative will open the hangar and let you out."

He let him go with a shove.

"I understand. Tell her." He took a deep breath. "Tell her I'm sorry."

"She already knows that." West looked down on him with indifference. "Be ready within the hour. I will be waiting just outside this door."

West left the room leaving him with the operatives.

Kevin nodded. When the operative left, he leaned forward until his face was deep in the covers and let out multiple yells. The tears he shed were soaked up by the bedding. He stayed like that for a long time, not having the motivation to get up yet. Finally spent, he forced himself to sit up and swung his legs off the side. With slow, meticulous moves, he undressed and donned the bodysuit.

Fully dressed, with a long leather coat over the body suit and vision goggles set atop his head, Kevin grabbed the bag. He walked out of the room then followed the operative down the hall. For the first time since the war, he was about to go outside.

CHAPTER TWO

THE TERRITORIES

Flat.

For as far as the eye could see. Nothing but barren, dry earth with the occasional petrified piece of debris sticking out. The still angry sky filtered the sunlight to cast an eerie brightness that felt artificial. There wasn't a creature in sight nor any plant life. Xander checked the display screen on the dash of his hovercraft. It showed the terrain fifty miles out from his position. The weather pattern would change once he reached the summit line.

He sat back in the driver seat and stretched his legs as it receded from the operating panel. The all-white interior with silver metal fixtures and black instrument gauges made him feel like he was trapped in a medical pod. The vehicle was actually equipped with one in the back. His black bodysuit hugged every inch of him, its material light enough to breath yet hard to damage with traditional weapons. He ran his hands across his abdomen, feeling the sleekness.

I hope you're as tough as they say, he thought referring to the suit and himself.

Footage collected from the archives were loaded in the vehicle's database. He watched them whenever he felt bored only to stop the feed midway, the content giving him anxiety. A lot of the small sectors populated with survivors gladly helped out travelers in need. Those coming to cause harm were met with extreme prejudice. Those tiny communities were not naïve. They had created strongholds.

It was the other sectors he worried about. There was no way to avoid some of them along the way and he needed to be mentally prepared. He had read text files on post-apocalyptic scenarios, fiction and non, describing a bleak, barbaric world of subhuman behavior. The current time was not as bad. He summed it up to the fact that not all of technology had not disappeared. Humans didn't have to start off from scratch to rebuild. But there also lay the problem. Those with technology either exploited it, used it for dominance, or kept it to themselves.

No trust anymore.

He glanced at the timing icons on the panel. Three hours until the summit. Ten percent solar charge. That feature was useless to even have operational given the lack of the sun's intensity. Four years, eight months, seven days, nine hours, twenty two minutes, and forty seconds left of cell battery. He snorted at that. He had no intention of being out in the territories that long. Dying was not an option and he vowed to be back home within a year's time.

The Litigator. He had also read up on what kind of being Senigrankes are. From the files, the alien race seemed similar to weather gods of folklore and ancient religions. Not a bad guy on the surface. Until you understand its origin. Thankfully, there was no footage of their kind consuming other species while hunting. For such predators to be so highly advanced, enough to open pathways across the galaxy as hunting grounds yet stay in a primitive mindset until evolving fascinated him.

His eyelids started to feel heavy. With so much time left until the next territory, he decided a short nap would do him some good. After the first sector in that area, he would encounter hostiles and he needed all the strength he could muster.

"Proximity alert!"

Startled, he sat up and stared out the front viewport. A huge black grid was bursting out of the ground directly ahead. He glanced at the counter and saw he had already passed the threshold of the first sector.

"Please brace for evasive maneuver."

He barely had time to steady himself as the vehicle swiveled sideways and traveled along the rising grid. More popped up as they went. Seeing what the grid's objective was, he sat correct in the seat and moved into up to the control panel.

"Initiate override sequence. Switch to manual mode," he ordered.

The vehicle obeyed and he took over. He could see the village off in the distance so hit the zoom icon on the screen. A small band of people were at an enclosed module working levels and buttons. He timed the grid's ascension at each section then sped up to beat it. Right before the next row popped out of the ground, he swerved ninety degrees and shot forward, the backside narrowly escaping. He watched the people up ahead scramble down the platform, weapons already out, and form a line in front of him. He came to a complete stop fifty feet away from them.

One of the people came forward with a small device in their hands. They raised it to their cloth covered mouth.

"This is a private sector. Turn back or be killed."

He snorted and hit the open channel.

"That's a little excessive, don't you think? Do you just murder anyone who passes through? From what I see, this is open space. No one owns anything out here. Or, are you merely remnants of the corruption that got us here?"

He heard a slight sputter and the device click off. The others on each side of the person turned to him and they began to converse amongst themselves. Finally the person held the device back up to his mouth and it clicked on.

"State the nature of your intent."

Making a loud sigh they could hear, he replied, "As I said the first time, I am passing through. Now move. I need to get to my destination on schedule."

There was hesitation from the group, each looking at the others.

Now what?

To his surprise, they began to approach his vehicle. When they had surrounded it, the one with the mini amplifier tapped on the driver side window.

"What are you doing?" He asked calmly through the open channel.

The person pulled down the cloth from their face, waved his weapon then holstered it. Xander lowered the window halfway. The man outside pursed his lips.

"The village on the other side of ours is not to be trifled with. You don't look prepared for that. This," he tapped on the side of the vehicle. "They would take this from you in a heartbeat."

"I appreciate the concern but already know about it. I don't plan on stopping."

"Did you plan to this time?" The man asked bluntly.

He stopped to think about that. The hidden grid system was genius and he had not known about it. There was no telling what the hostile village beyond had in their arsenal.

"So, what do you propose?" He asked.

"You follow us to our village. We will scan you and your vehicle for any pathogens then send you on your way come dawn."

"Not many visitors to entertain these days, huh?" Xander laughed then stopped as the man pulled his weapon back out and pointed it at him.

"Don't be a smart ass, kid. Get moving. Never kick a gift horse in the mouth."

"What?" He started to ask what the hell that meant when one of the other people tapped the other side of the vehicle. The eyes were mere slits, but he could see the anger in them.

"Fine. Lead the way."

He raised the window back up and relaxed in his seat as he disabled the channel.

"Resume operations," he spoke to the vehicle. The quiet engine engaged, the control panel showing it as running. "Follow at pace."

The vehicle eased out as the group headed towards the village. He shook his head, not quite sure if it was a trap or they were really worried about him.

The group came to an entry twenty feet high and twice as wide. The center split open enough to allow them to go in single file. Barely visible behind the corners of the wall on the other side were armed lookouts wrapped up to combat the elements. An enemy would encounter a world of hurt because they would not have seen them until getting inside.

The vehicle eased through and the wall closed behind it. Even covered head to toe, he could see the scattered inhabitants along the road were not happy to see an outsider. At the end of the main street, his escorts turned left and he followed. Another street emerged and this time a one level grey building sat up ahead.

Scorch marks covered the sides with a few pieces broken off near the top. Small antennas were attached and positioned towards the sky. There were no windows that he could see. Two guards stood on either side of what must have been the entrance. There was nothing to distinguish it, not even the outlines of a frame.

Flashing strobe lights came on and lines appeared in the middle section of the building between the guards. They expanded until there was indeed a frame line. The entire section dissolved like a hologram and revealed a hangar converted into a communication and operations center. Consoles were along the walls with a main long board in the center. One of the men got his attention and pointed to an area where combat fighter planes would have docked. Parking his vehicle on the platform, he got out.

"This way," the man ordered tersely.

Before the men working in the building could get to the vehicle, it sealed itself up. One of the men stopped a few feet short of it then turned to him.

"Open it back up!"

"No." He stared them all down.

The scout leader let a loud sigh.

"Why won't you cooperate?"

"There is no reason for anyone to be inside the vehicle during a scan. You going to try to dissect me when I go through as well?"

A handful of his escorts readied their weapons, aiming them at his head. The scout leader raised a hand and they lowered them.

"Fair enough." He motioned to a tech nearby. "Do the scan and leave it there." To Xander he stepped to the side and held out an arm. "This way."

He followed the two techs ahead of him and noticed two more took up the rear while the leader kept at his side. Behind an enclosed examination room sat a full body scanner equipped with surgical apparatus. He raised his eyebrows at the scout leader.

"You don't need to strip," the scout leader said, exasperated. "Get in." To the operator sitting at the controls he said, "Scan only. Full range of detection."

The doors slid open and he went inside. He looked over the machine, taking in the advanced technology derived from the aliens. There was a clearing of the throat and he got the hint, climbing into the scanner and lying down. The hatch closed and a cold smoke filled the chamber until it could not be seen through. He could see lines of light playing across his body. The smoke cleared as he heard soft suction all around him.

"Scanning complete," the other tech announced.

The hatch opened but as he went to sit up, straps shot out from the sides and held him down. He struggled to get lose.

"Stay still! We need to go over the data before we let you out," the tech said.

"Then you should have told me that."

Xander laid back.

"Well?" The scout leader asked the tech.

The tech frowned before replying, "He's clean. Pristine, even. Not even one pathogen detected."

"That can't be. The levels of crud outside alone would attach to him and create something." The scout leader went to the tech's side.

"Because I've never been out in the open yet," he said.

Both men looked up at him in awe. The scout leader leaned forward.

"You mean to tell me you have kept yourself inside that vehicle the whole time?"

He turned his head to him.

"That's correct."

"Wouldn't hurt him even if he did," the tech stated. "His immune system is off the charts. I don't think anything would get past it."

The straps rescinded into the sides of the scanner to let him finally get up. He exited the room and stood next to the control board for further instructions. The scout leader walked past him and gestured for him to come with.

They went down a long corridor lit up with glow orbs above. The whole interior of the building was the same color as it was outside; dull and grey. Bright light flooded the hall as they approached the end of the hall. Beyond the threshold was a sprawling array of tiny makeshift homes and green houses. The people were in regular robes and bodysuits, not wrapped up to the gills like his escorts. He looked up and saw they were under a large dome connected to the building. Artificial sunlight gave the entire area an outdoor, country feel. The dome was not visible when he came upon the territory earlier. As if seeing his dilemma, the scout leader explained.

"We are actually below the main level. No reason for anyone to see what we really got."

He merely nodded, still enchanted by the vastness of the environment. Though it only housed maybe a few thousand people, the place was teeming with activity. There were field workers, patrollers, construction workers and technicians all doing tasks.

"This way."

The scout leader walked off and led the way to a house larger than the rest. Inside was an open eating area with people prepping food on stainless steel counters along the perimeter. Each station had a different task. Vegetables were being chopped with actual knives and there was a woman holding what looked like a mini blow torch over a large pan.

"Those of us on duty, come here to relax and get fed. We go back out every four to eight hours depending on rotation. When one group comes in, another goes out in its place."

"Efficient." He nodded in approval.

"Looks like meatloaf today," one of the escorts said.

"Not real meat, of course," he stated, then looked over at the scout leader. "Unless there's something you need to tell me about missing enemies."

The escort's face turned a darker shade as his face scrunched up.

"We don't eat people! It's plant-based protein!"

He raised his hands in defense, stepping back in case the man came at him. The scout leader pursed his lips and gave him a side glance. Around them, the preppers had stopped to give him dirty looks as well.

"I haven't been out here," he began. "There's no telling what goes on."

A large man came out from behind a door at the end. He wasn't all wrapped up like the other men, wearing a long, light brown dingy robe over a battlesuit. His hair was past his shoulders and he had full beard.

"He's right. We know of a few sectors that do just that. Can't blame him for jumping to conclusions." He extended a hand to Xander. "I am the leader of this territory. Not sure if you're brave or stupid for travelling out here."

"Neither," he answered, shaking the man's hand. "Simply on a mission."

"Well, take a breather, get some food and rest. You're going to need it."

The leader cocked his head to one side and stared at the entourage behind Xander.

"Is there a reason why you are all still swathed in cloth inside the gates?"

For the first time, Xander saw them all look embarrassed. The scout leader made a face and began to unwind the fabric around his head and neck.

"Just forgot," he mumbled as the others did the same.

The man let out a hearty laugh.

"They were trying to intimidate you, I suppose."

"Didn't work. It takes a lot to get me nervous."

The man stared at him, seeming to take stock of him.

"Bioengineered. Combat class. I know that physique."

Xander took a step back from him. As much as he wanted to hide his fear, it came through in his eyes. The man's expression turned to empathy.

"It's not something to be ashamed of." The man held out a hand. "It means someone took great care in creating you. Bioengineered doesn't mean not human. I'm pretty sure you have an actual parent who decided not to carry you herself but use an incubator."

He clenched his hands into fists. That was true. Yet, it still stung.

"Let's get settled," the scout leader interrupted. "Food is almost ready."

He turned around and nearly fell sideways as he saw the scout leader sans rags. Dark blonde hair in a short, butchered cut was sticking out all over a slightly tanned face. His eyes were what surprised him. Blue irises with gold rimmed around them narrowed at being scrutinized.

"Sorry," he mumbled, regaining his balance.

"Whatever," the scout leader replied.

While the others took seats at the benches, the territory leader smiled, slapping Xander on the back.

"Did you forget who was left behind to keep fighting after evacuations during the war? Come on. Eat."

The man threw an arm around his neck and ushered him to an empty seat at the middle table. He caught a glimpse of the giant pan of fake meatloaf coming out. It looked amazing. Like it came right out from a cooking show from the early days. Chunks of fresh green onions, potatoes, and tomatoes could be seen within the dark brown mass. The peaks had a crusty blackness from being hit with a flaming torch, making some of the oils rise and glisten.

It's not real meat, he told himself again but had to admit, it sure looked like it.

After dinner, he was escorted to a small living quarter with four bunk beds. The cushions assembled to create a mattress seemed barely used. There was a tiny window near the ceiling that showed the false sky.

"This group is out scouting. They won't return until the next shift. I suggest you get some rest before heading back out." The scout leader said.

"Why can't I leave now?" He asked.

"I wouldn't recommend it. At this time of day, the next territory over does some pretty nasty stuff."

"And you do nothing to stop it."

An air of hostility covered the room. The scout leader's hands balled into fists.

"We won't help those who have no intention of helping themselves."

The leader of the territory came up from behind him and laid a hand on his shoulder. The scout leader relaxed and un-balled his hands.

"Although there are some people who are victims inside that sector, the majority revel in the festivities. We did try to remedy the situation and were met with contempt for meddling."

"They attacked in retaliation?" Xander asked.

"Of course." The leader smiled. "And they have never tried that again."

Xander understood the implication. He had no doubt this territory was armed to the teeth. They didn't flaunt its might. He walked further into the room and stood in the center.

"Thank you for your wisdom and hospitality."

"May I ask," the leader came beside him. "Where are you going in such a hurry?"

"To negotiate with the Litigator."

He heard gasps behind him.

"That's an impossible mission."

"I don't think so. He is an intelligent being. I'm sure he can see reason."

"He has no obligation to repair this planet."

"He has no intention of doing that." Xander turned his head towards the leader and they locked in a stare. The leader's eyes narrowed as he understood.

"This is a dangerous gamble."

"We know."

"Rest. You're going to need it," the leader tossed over his shoulder as he left the room.

The rest of the group moved down the hall, leaving him alone. He let out a loud sigh and plopped on the closest bottom bunk. His body sank and it felt like he was floating on a cloud. Exhaustion took hold of him. He had kept his composure the whole time even though he had been in defense mode. His body relented to the softness as he drifted off. Come tomorrow, he would have to prepare to fight his way through the next sector.

A small hand pressed against his chest and shook him. Xander opened his eyes and was met with an angry little boy of maybe eight years old. He wore a long-sleeved tunic and combat pants rolled up at the ankles. His feet were bare and his hair a tussled mess. Across his shoulder was an old school assault rifle.

"You're in my bed," the boy huffed. "I need to sleep."

"Sorry." Xander sat up with hands raised in the air. He swung his legs over the edge of the bed and stood. The boy stared up at him in awe. "They let me sleep here until you got back. It's nice and warm for you."

His face regained the frown as he looked away. He took the rifle off and laid it on the far side of the bed then climbed in.

"Whatever. Better hurry or you'll miss breakfast."

"What about you? Aren't you going to eat?"

Xander turned around and saw the boy was already asleep, arms curled around the rifle. He didn't like the sight of that one bit. One of the scouts from the previous shift came and nodded for him to follow.

They walked back to the mess hall and he was hit with savory and sweet aromas. He caught a glimpse of the food. Pancakes with fraudulent sausage. Then he thought about it logically. The pancakes weren't made from tradition flour either. Nonetheless, both looked and smelled delicious. A row of pitchers filled with a thick liquid sat on a table adjacent to the chow line. He figured it must be some type of protein drink.

The two loaded their trays with breakfast and sat at a far bench seat.

"Ready to go?" The scout who escorted him asked.

"As much as I can be."

The man's face turned serious and he pointed a finger.

"Be careful. If you feel for one moment that it can get ugly, high tail your ass out of there and don't look back."

"They won't chase me?" Xander asked surprised.

"Oh, they will. But only for a few kilometers if that vehicle of yours outpaces them."

"Good to know."

"Eat up. I have to get you back to the hangar before the sun breaks the horizon."

"What happens at the beak of dawn?"

The escort merely smiled.

"Don't worry about it. Just know, you need to be gone."

They finished eating and without pause, Xander was lead back the way they came to the where his vehicle was waiting. All the scouts along with the leader stood silent witness as he opened the hatch and settled into the driver seat. The scout leader tossed a package to him and he caught it with one hand.

"What's this?" The scout leader frowned. Xander took a sniff then nodded in approval. "Hmm. Thanks. I'll save it for after I get through the other side."

"Safe journey," the territory leader said. There was apprehension in his voice.

Xander closed the hatch and started the engine. The hangar doors opened and two vehicles similar to his sat blocking the pathway. The first began to move and he followed, the other coming up behind him. They made the slow and steady procession through the main streets, the people again giving him dirty looks as he passed.

At the wall, the two vehicles moved to each side of his and waited for it to open. When there was enough room for him to go through, the guard atop the edge waved him on. He eased the vehicle out into the dusty landscape. After getting a good distance away, he looked through the rear camera view and saw the entire compound start to grow dim, blending into the sand and sky.

Camouflage.

He had never noticed it before and chided himself for not realizing sooner. It was the reason why he had not seen the structure on approach the first time. Laughing out loud, he set the vehicle back to autopilot.

"Resume destination," he commanded.

"Recalculating timetable. New arrival time established."

He adjusted the seat back and tapped the display screen. His education feed was still paused so he hit the play icon. A warning message came on the screen stating the file was top secret and property of the United States of America. That meant nothing now. He brought his knees up and rested his feet on the dash as more information about the Litigator played.

WAITING ROOM

Roland sat atop a mountain in what used to be Japan while looking out at the horizon. The sky was an array of colors cascading across the planet causing weather anomalies. Storms of every kind popped up every few weeks depending on the region, including acid rain.

I could fix this.

During the last moments of the war, he had expressed a desire to wipe out all humans and let the planet heal itself. It came down as an unpopular solution. Nevertheless, he still had that in mind as he watched the territories emerge over the past decade. Some of the people merely wanted to survive. Others sought out conquest.

Case in point; those former power-hungry world leaders who decided a new world order was necessary. He observed their reign of terror ramp up the past couple of years. When he was still filming for a reality television show, humans nauseated him regardless if their intentions were good. They were a uniquely flawed species that he couldn't understand.

And now a group of them were coming to plead their case, persuade him not to do what he recommended. Of course, he knew the world leaders had another idea in store. He wondered what method they found that guaranteed his demise. The only species known to kill a Senigranke was another Senigranke.

How naïve.

He stood, brushing off the makeshift wide legged pants he created from discarded fabric found in an abandoned bunker. They were lightweight and breathable, allowing him to move freely if needed. His shirt was of a more flowing material and hung past his waist. Seeing so many of the warriors left on the planet still wearing their battle suits was a turn off. He preferred comfort and had no need for such constricting attire.

"Now, what shall I do to prepare for my guests' arrival?"

Down below was barren land, dusty and spanning nearly five miles. He smiled.

"Ah, I will make a territory of my own."

The Book of Litigation appeared before him floating at chest level and surrounded by a pastel green glow. His eyes glowed the same color as the pages flipped on their own until stopping a third way in. The sky above revealed the bloody sun and the ground opened, tossing the caked terrain as if being plowed. Murky clouds converged and dirty rain moistened the surface.

"Yes, come," he said referring to the group heading his way. "I will hear you out." Then he grinned. "Maybe."

On the vidscreen, an armed New Order unit attacked a hostile town in one of the most violent territories and stopped short of obliterating it. They had come for the town's most precious asset: a satellite tower that still functioned despite its range being shortened due to the sky. The noncombatants were rounded up in the center of the town and microchipped while its previous leaders ended up dead or in cages. All of it took less than two hours.

Impressive, Chad Hoskins thought.

No longer a general and deemed an enemy of humanity, he had been lying in wait for the dust to clear after the battle. When the evacuations were announced, he knew right off the bat that he wasn't going. He saw all those candy asses scramble to get aboard a ship to take them away from all the hardship war entailed. Even the Terror who acted as his personal bodyguard up and abandoned him for the nearest transport.

He had grown a full beard but kept his hair short and not so tight. Grooming was secondary in the current times. His combat uniform had seen better days and his boots were starting to hurt his feet. The tailor would have to start making new pieces soon. A newly acquired manufacturing machine was going to be put to use.

He had set up operations in a military installation he purchased long before the battle. Inside the bunkeresque structure was a fully functional communications center and a navigation system that auto-updated. Getting an accurate map of the territories was key to his new plan.

"Excuse me, sir."

He turned to see Jesse, his father's informant from the early days standing next to him. The man was almost unrecognizable with long scraggly hair, sunken eyes and all lean muscle. Despite having alien DNA that slowed aging to a crawl, Jesse appeared twenty years older. Hardened with eyes that had seen too much. Chad had made sure to put him to work after his father turned him loose.

"Whatcha' got there?"

Jesse's eyes narrowed as he caught a glimpse of the holoscreen.

"Reports of the sites the New Order is targeting."

"Oh yeah? And where are they off to next?"

"It's a matter of when and how. Apparently, there's a

facility still above surface. They want to hit it hard."

"Those fuckers have no idea what they're doing. You need a hell of a plan and an insider to take one of those things down." Chad swiveled in his chair towards him. "Whose is it?"

"Headland."

"The Australian broad?" He asked incredulously.

"It seems they tried to," Jesse put his fingers up in quotations, "negotiate, with her."

Chad burst out laughing, startling the others in the room. When finished, his expression turned ugly.

"New Order my ass!" He met Jesse's gaze. "Find out where the other facilities are. Most of the oceans have either dried up or low level. They would be exposed."

Jesse raised his brow. "We going to hit them first?"

"You bet your sweet little ass we are. Those New Order freaks are just going to bring back the same old society structure everyone rejected when it was in place the first time. No, we need to start over with something different."

"You're willing to embrace the hybrids now?"

Chad gave him a vicious stare.

"Not even. They'll be isolated like they should have been."

"The New Order has maps to weapons locations."

"You mean the ones we have under our command?"

"Yeah, those. They figure they could just come through and take what they need."

"They'll be in for a rude awakening. Use your network. Find those facilities."

"On it."

As Jesse left through the sliding door, Chad caught a glimpse of the high-powered handgun tucked in the back of the man's cargo pants at the waist.

Jesse the informant turned guerilla killer.

Chad let out another laugh.

Priceless.

⌒

Reinhart sat in the meeting room alone swiveling his chair back and forth while he watched a live feed on the tabletop. His thumb was hooked under his chin with his forefinger rested against the side of his face. An expression of deep thought covered it. He tapped the image with his free hand to zoom in on the group of assailants surrounding one of the prized weapons bunkers. The way they moved with such efficiency screamed military. More distinctly, like a Terror cover formation. Whenever a Terror was about to be unleashed, a ground unit would lay the foundation for the carnage to come.

Alarms went off in his head.

Of all the people to survive, he was certain Chad Hoskins was back in play. That was the last thing the New Order needed. A narcissist who didn't work well with others of authority. A rogue. His counterpart, Jankowski, came into the room and sat next to him at the table. He turned, eyes narrowed and pointed to the image.

"Guess who's come to dinner?"

Jankowski leaned over the image and squinted.

"A new faction of rebels?"

"Look closer."

After a few seconds, he sucked air through his teeth and leaned back.

"Can't be! That bastard!"

"What bastard?" Omar asked as he entered.

"Hoskins," Jankowski sneered.

"So he's alive. What's he up to?"

"Hitting a weapons compound," Reinhart replied softly. He glanced up at them.

"Goddamn it!" Jankowski's face scrunched. "That

can't be the only thing he's after. Is this the first time we've seen this group?"

"As far as we know, yes."

"He may be trying to do the exact same thing as us," Omar added.

"And this is why we need a long-range communication network. The only reason we know about this is because it is within our fifty-mile range." Jankowski spat.

"Which, in my opinion is too close. That means he knows where we are." Omar rested his elbows on the table. "We should send out a defense unit to the next site."

"Agreed." Jankowski removed his hand from his face and laid them flat. He drummed his fingers on the hard surface. "Hoskins, you fucker."

"Let's not lose our heads." Omar chided.

"Yes. I say two or three cannon units should suffice." Reinhart suggested.

"First, we need to know his next target." Jankowski said.

"That's easy. If he's that close, the next would be the one sitting all alone in the desert with no shelter. He probably thinks it a prime steal." Omar replied.

Reinhart raised his tablet and scrolled through his database. Finding the coordinates, he relayed them to his section leader. He tapped the commlink icon.

"Do we have any units already nearby that we can reroute? I'd hate to deploy another before the last group gets back."

The section leader's voice crackled.

"There are two around the area. I can get another one to connect in the next day or two."

"Good." Reinhart frowned. "Why is the reception bad? You're breaking up."

"Storm. Looks bad. We are going to have to hunker

down in the vehicles for about twelve hours. Radio silence."

"Stay safe out there."

"Roger that, sir.

The connection died and Omar had a stern look.

"This weather thing is hindering our progress. The Litigator could easily have fixed this."

"Or he's the cause," Reinhart added.

⌇

Drops of water echoed in the cave set deep in the mountain crevice. Muted sunlight creeped halfway in unable to reach beyond the darkness permeating the rest of it path. Two bodies wrapped in thermal sleeping bags lay side by side, their breaths drifting up in the cold air. Behind them were a stockpile of provisions, a quarter of it acquired over the years. The first person stirred, wiggling part way out of their sleep bag. Hair black as pitch sat in disarray on their head, covering their face. They blew hard against it revealing pale skin.

Gragor let out a loud yawn and leaned forward, not daring to push the sleep bag completely off. It was colder than usual. The climate was trying to regulate itself. Being so far up in the mountains meant ice and snow were coming back. He looked out to the opening lit by peach colored sunlight.

What a mess.

"Bree." He called out softly. The other sleeping bag rolled on its side. "Time to get up. We have to go down again today." There was a muffled reply. "What'd you say?" He nudged the bag. "Get up."

The top of the bag opened, and Bree's head peeked out. A hand gripped the edge, keeping it from opening further. Jet black hair formed a web around his head.

"Is that supposed to be an order?"

His voice was hoarse from the cold.

"Don't."

He could see Bree's slatted eyes through parted strands of his hair. They were full of discontent. That didn't matter. Bree needed to get his ass in gear.

"Fine." Bree came out of the bag up to his waist. "Why are we going down?"

"We have an intervention to plan."

"Fravral is looking for you."

Bree turned his attention to the small device taken from Gragor's combat ship before it was destroyed. Its digital display showed coordinates from a downed Relliant escape ship.

"He'll have to wait a little longer. We didn't go through all this so that meddling Litigator could wipe it out on a whim."

"Agreed."

Bree pushed the rest of the sleeping bag off and stood. He raised his arms in the air and stretched. His combat suit was opened down to his midriff exposing the healed wound from battle. It was a dark, rusty red splotch with tiny lines running through it like veins. Bree scratched it a few times before pulling the suit's fabric back together. The nanobots within made quick work of closing it, the material now seamless.

Not to be seen as a hypocrite, Gragor reluctantly slid out of his sleeping bag. His combat suit was off at the waist, the sleeves bunched up near his thighs. The cold hit him instantly and he hurried to pull it back on. Both men ran their fingers through their hair to tame it.

"So, what breakfast feast are we having today?"

Bree eyed the sack in the corner.

When they retrieved their rations from both ships, they were the size of large boulders filled with meats and staples of food from their planet. At least ten years' worth. Now there was only one left and it was half empty even though they had been rationing it out. There was maybe another two years of supplies left.

"Hmm. Meat and starches." Gragor quipped. "Or," he raised a finger in pause. "Meat and starches." Bree made a face. "Be thankful. This is a luxury. Earth has no wildlife or plants on its surface. You saw what some of the humans have resorted to."

Cannibalism.

Not unusual by any means. Senigrankes ate beings all the time. And they were not the only species to do so. For some reason, seeing humans go down that route was jarring. Unnatural.

The two sat on rocks they had positioned around another to create an eating area. Gragor undid the fastener on the bag and pulled out a small packet of preserved meat. He broke it in half and tossed one to Bree. From a container with rows of mini trays, he slid out two and handed them out. Bree sighed, shoulders slumped then sat straight and pulled the film off the tray. A beige gruel shimmied inside. They ate in silence, gathering their resolve.

"If Fravral is looking for you, why is his signature going the wrong way?"

Gragor looked up from his meal and gave Bree a sideways glance.

"That is odd. Maybe he's being pursued?"

Bree's eyes became hooded.

"More like he's found some prey more fascinating than rendezvousing with you."

"That could be." Gragor went stiff. "If he has those Cyboks with him."

Bree frowned. As much as he loathed what humans had become after the war, he didn't want to see them up against a Cybok at this stage. Gragor pointed down.

"Come on. Finish eating. We have to go before the weather does that thing again."

"I think it's Roland messing up things and having fun."

"All the more reason we have to get to him before those new order people. I really don't want to see a slaughter. They are no match for him."

"Unless they've found a way."

Gragor slurped the last of his gruel and stood, staring down at Bree with a dubious smirk.

"Really?"

They inserted their trash in the portable incinerator and donned their gear for traveling the outside. View goggles, a heavy coat, nutrient drinks and weapons. Their guns were attached to the side of their thighs and the drinks in a small satchel on their backs. They walked out of the cave they had claimed as home for the past eight years into daylight.

And there were New Order units down below. One group had a handheld signature locator and its leader was pointing up towards them. When the man locked eyes with Bree, he seemed to panic, tapping his associates. Bree counted twenty men in the unit. Recon. He turned to Gragor who smiled.

"Well, can't have them bringing friends, now can we?"

Gragor stepped onto the ledge.

"I'm going." Bree leapt off.

He dove the kilometer down to a horrified group of humans staring up at him. The roof of the white vehicle opened and a cannon rose out. It swiveled until the targeting system found Bree and fired. Without a flinch, Bree continued his dive, dodging the round by tilting his body slightly to one side.

His eyes glowed bright blue as his hands sliced the air in front of him. A blue arc came down on the vehicle splitting it and the cannon in half. The men inside scrambled out right as it exploded while the ones already outside opened fire. Bree pulled both of his guns and shot down eight of the enemy in quick succession. He landed as if stepping down a set of stairs.

One of the New Order men ran the opposite way, a communicator in his hand.

"Emergency! We're being engaged by hostile entities. Requesting…"

The back of the man's head splayed apart. Gragor came from the rocky edge gun leveled. He snatched the communicator from the man's grip before the body hit the ground. With one squeeze, Gragor crushed the device. The firing ceased. What remained of the group stood in fear realizing they were stranded with no way to get back except on foot.

"What do you want to do with them?" Bree asked.

"Well, that depends." Gragor turned to the survivors and his eyes glowed. "If the information we get is worthy of them staying alive."

The New Order person closest to Gragor looked up and gave him a stare full of malice. Gragor gave him one back, followed with a grin.

TO CATCH A THIEF

Although not bright the sun still kicked out a decent amount of heat. The square building covered in scorch marks sat alone with nothing around it for miles. as the rooftop became superheated. It appeared small on the outside but in actuality was a behemoth covering over twenty thousand square feet. Inside, the space was sectioned off for communications, weapons storage, and provisions. A hangar at the far wall led to a lower level where vehicles were housed.

Armed guards walked the area while the vidscreens above displayed a view of the outside from every angle. There would be no surprise attacks. In the center lay the communications console where Hoskins sat patiently waiting for some action to take place. He had gotten wind of the New Order's plan to hit the installation and retrieve more territory.

But this one is mine, you bastards. Hands off.

His crew was no more than a hundred and forty strong, yet they packed a punch when it came to defending what Hoskins asked them to. The number shocked him when he tallied up who had stayed behind. He was sure only a handful, like twenty or so, would follow his lead. It almost got downright hostile the first couple years holed up together in that bunker he purchased from a rogue scientist right before the shit hit the fan. Personalities clashed along with opinions on if going out and fighting was an obligation or plain stupid. They could feel the ground shifting with each blast and over time, the thing was obviously slanted.

On the screen to his left he saw something white glint in the horizon. A few more popped around and he could see them getting bigger; closer. The New Order was coming to show their faces. Hoskins swiveled in his chair and punched the PA button.

"Get ready people. The enemy is afoot."

A soldier came up to him, rifle slung over one shoulder.

"Want us to meet them outside?"

Hoskins tilted his head and thought for a moment.

"Hmm. Let 'em get kind of close before opening the front door. As far as they can tell, the place hasn't been breached."

"Got it, sir."

The soldier went off to relay the plan to the rest of his unit. Jesse came out of the back hangar and strode to the communication center. His hair was pulled back in a ponytail that didn't hold it all. Strands fell forward against the sides of his face as he leaned over the console.

"I zoomed in and saw a few land air weapons. Signatures running hot."

"So, they're ready to rock and roll, huh?"

"Moving in tactical formations under the assumption we are close behind them."

"Never occurred to them that I was here first?" Hoskins squinted with a smirk.

"Apparently not. They were too busy focused on that weapons compound raid a couple of weeks ago."

"I'll say it again. Amateurs."

Jankowski's assistant stood at the helm of the first vehicle watching the pilots navigate towards the installation. It was not the first time they had come to it for supplies and he was always amazed it hadn't been touched in all that time. Now he had to deal with Hoskins trying to get his grubby hands on it. The New Order had a solid agenda. He could almost guarantee the former general was up to no good, vowing to bring back chaos.

"Turn on infrared scanners and search the area. I want to know when that son of a bitch shows up with his horde of heathens."

The first pilot leaned back in awe with brow raised at the assistant's words. His copilot's mouth went downward, pursing his lips. He switched on the scanners as they got within a quarter mile from the installation and the screens above went orange.

"Oh shit!" He yelled.

"Stop the convoy!" The assistant ordered through the commlink attached to his ear. He looked at the screen showing signatures throughout the inside of the installation. "That sneaky..." He tapped the copilot. "Open a channel. I want to talk to that bastard."

"Opening communication link."

Hoskins nearly spit out the sip of drink he had taken from his canteen when he saw the commlink blink.

"Is he for real?"

"Want me to connect?" His communications officer asked.

"Sure."

On the middle vidscreen came the flushed angry face of the assistant. His white jacket was pristine, nearly glowing. His mouth seemed to struggle with what expression to take on then settled on a fake closed lipped smile.

"Hoskins, you are not authorized to occupy this installation. It is under the protection of the New World Order. We insist that you vacate the premises immediately. If, upon acceptance into the faction, you need shelter, we can accommodate you at one of our other facilities."

Hoskins burst out laughing, nearly falling out of his seat as he leaned too far back. Even Jesse snorted and had to cover his mouth to stop the giggling.

"Ahhh!" Hoskins sat back upright and exhaled. "Oh man, that is gold!"

"I am being very serious," the assistant spat.

"Well, you have a big misunderstanding. You see, this here installation was bought by me way before that little war started. And I sure as shit didn't give you dipshits permission to take from it, let alone claim ownership in my absence."

"Things have changed, Hoskins. The world needs leadership to steer it in the right direction. You only want to stir things up."

"Wrong." Hoskins' eyes narrowed. "I am going to do what should have been done in the first place. You asshats are only looking for power."

"I will only give you one last warning."

The vehicle with the land to air weapons turned around so the cannons faced the installation.

"You know what I found interesting," Hoskins began. "The lower level of the hangar had never been accessed."

"What does that have to do with anything?" The assistant turned his head to the right. "Fire the first shot. Target the center."

"Jesse," Hoskins said.

"On it." Jesse went over to a different section and began typing on a console. "Defense weapons online.

Bringing main gun to surface."

They both watched the assistant's face contort into horror as the main gun rose up from behind the building and fire on the incoming blast from the vehicle's cannon. The two shots collided, sending bursts of white and yellow that blinded both sides. As it died out, the assistant's face scrunched up with rage.

"I warned you!" The assistant's hostile tone carried through the feed.

The connection was severed, and Hoskins saw more vehicles come into view. Groups of armed people in white flooded out of them.

"Incoming." The ops officer announced.

"No shit," Hoskins replied sarcastically. A laser blast shot a three-inch hole through the wall near ops. Sunlight peeked in. "What do you think?"

The twenty-foot doors began to open, and the first combat unit went out to greet the New Order faction. Laser fire crisscrossed the terrain while the large white vehicles with cannons moved into position forming an arc around the building. Hoskins got up and headed towards the hangar. Jesse caught up to him and set a hand on his shoulder.

"Let us have some fun. You sit back and watch."

"Oh yeah?" Hoskins turned to him. "You going out?"

"Sure am."

Jesse jogged to the back door and hit the card reader with his keycard. The wall slid open revealing the steep concrete ramp that went down into darkness. Light flicked on illuminating the space and dozens of vehicles sat in rows along the floor. Similar to the ones the New Order used, these were military grade with better mobility and more weapons.

"Show 'em whatcha got." Hoskins gave him a wave and headed back to his seat. "Bring that chicken shit out if you can. I wanna give him a piece of my mind."

"If he refuses?"

"Shoot him." Hoskins stopped. "Better yet, drag his ass in here. I'll shoot him."

Jesse laughed as he strode down the ramp followed by a combat unit. Hoskins knew what that meant. The man was about to go full ballistic. He wondered if it stemmed from his father throwing him to the curve or seeing a dysfunctional bureaucracy at work up close. Either way, he had gained a loyal comrade. Hoskins put his feet up and grabbed his canteen. Taking a swig, he leaned back to watch the vidscreens.

NEW COMPANIONS

Grannalt stood cautious in the open area staring at the pristine white vehicle unmoving up ahead. He couldn't figure out how the thing never got dirty from traveling across the territories until he zoomed in on the alloy the thing was made out of. He had seen it before being manufacture in one of the other countries' facility. The design was sleek and functional which he liked. Despite that, the thing stood out like a beacon.

He decided to take a chance and advanced towards it. At the one-hundred-yard mark, the vehicle lights came on.

"Warning. Further approach will initiate defense protocols. Please reverse course."

Grannalt recognized that annoying AI voice from the cannon system. He rolled his eyes in exasperation.

"Is anyone in there? Can you hear me? I am not an enemy," he yelled. He raised his hands up to reiterate his claim as the external minicams protruded out for a better view. "Are you lost? Need help?" He moved closer.

"Warning! Defense protocol initiating in…"

"Oh, shut up! Override command Alpha zero two seven Delta. Code Grandfather."

He hated that code. It was given to him out of spite due to his age in Earth years.

"Status. Protocol conflict."

"If you don't open that hatch, I will relay a kill switch."

There was a long pause.

"Command accepted. Opening hatch."

Grannalt pursed his lips, approaching the vehicle. The hatch opened and he peered into the cockpit and saw no one. A hand slapped against the side of the panel behind the drive seat and Grannalt nearly jumped out. He calmed himself, climbing farther in to see who was there. In the back section, hooked up to the medical unit was a young man barely conscious. His eyes were bloodshot and glazed over from pain killers doing their job.

"Who?" Was all he could get out. His hand slid down and lay limp.

"Oh damn. What happened to you?" He turned to the dash and addressed the AI. "When did this occur?"

"Five days, seven hours, twenty-two minutes and eight seconds have past."

"How far away?"

"Seventy-two kilometers."

"How long at this location?"

"Five days, three hours…"

"Never mind. Delay that response." He stroked the young man's forehead. "Prognosis."

"Severe damage to internal organs, deep lacerations, head trauma. Repair is at sixty percent. Full recovery in fifty hours. Patient still unable to sustain consciousness for longer than two minutes."

"What's his name?"

"Primary operator designation Xander Headland. Combat class. Fourth Gen."

Grannalt sucked air through his teeth. Creating bio-engineered children with compatible DNA was all the rage amongst the scientists in the first decades of his race's arrival. Modified humans to continue on their legacy.

The wind picked up and Grannalt could smell rain. He saw the dashboard light up and the weather tracker appeared. Not just rain. A massive storm full of sleet and debris.

"Storm approaching in one hour."

"Close hatch and prep for impact."

He noticed Xander was not strapped in securely and summated the kid had got himself into the unit in a hurry while commanding the vehicle to take off. Finding them all, Grannalt repositioned him and made sure each strap was tight enough to keep him in place without constriction. That storm looked ugly. It would lift the vehicle off the ground.

For the next forty-five minutes, Grannalt familiarized himself with the vehicle, arguing with the AI regarding protocol and yet again threatening to use the kill switch. He didn't want to do that because it would wipe out all the data. Finally, she gave up the goods and showed him the destination.

"Why there?"

"Location is last known detection of the Litigator."

Granalt let his head fall back and he stared at the overhead. He shook his head before bringing it up to look at the display. Certain the kid's mission was folly, he leaned against the seat and contemplated forcing a reroute. As if reading his mind, the kid's eyes opened. He reached out with one hand.

"Don't. Please."

His voice was barely a whisper, full of pain.

The vehicle began to rock. Grannalt looked out the window and saw a giant black funnel, squat in nature with a wide girth. Its top was a gaping hollow void. Not a tornado, something else; something new.

"Holy shit!"

The funnel slammed into the vehicle, pushing it into

the side of the bluff and carrying it upwards. He could hear the alloy scraping the rock. It would be pristine no more.

"Warning. Outer integrity critical."

"You better hold together!"

There was a loud ping like metal popping then…

Silence.

Grannalt watched horrified as the vehicle was flung out from the funnel's grip and went airborne. The calculation on the dash showed them rising fast enough to break the clouds in the next few seconds. The bluff below was now the size of a thumbnail. Then Grannalt remembered something about when the vehicle was manufactured.

"Initiate aerial configuration."

"Vehicle is not at optimal position to …"

The vehicle had stopped ascending and went into free fall.

"Correct position and do as I command!"

Another long pause. She was angry. The vehicle jerked thirty degrees to a flat position.

"Trajectory corrected. Initiating aerial configuration."

Extreme turbulence assaulted them as they got closer to the dissipating funnel moving steady across the plain beneath them. The vehicle bounced as wings expanded out from each side and thrusters engaged. The G force knocked Grannalt back into the seat, pinning him down. He managed to take a glimpse of Xander before his body was immobilized.

Out cold.

Grannalt took control of the vehicle as it landed, the wings folding back into the body. He hit the button to reconfigure it to surface mode, not ready to hand it over to the AI. There was silence behind him, and he was thankful for that. From the screen displaying the medical section, he could see the intravenous tubes full of liquid making its way into the kid's veins. The digital readout had the name of it above. A unique mixture of painkiller and sedative was slowly being pumped into him.

Turning his attention back to the road ahead, he found the terrain vastly different than the one they had left. What used to be mountains were now scattered in chunks along the way. Still majestic in their condensed size, they demanded acknowledgement by the way their positions created a winding pathway. Grannalt felt a bit of sadness for them. Iridescent snow clung to the tops making them appear otherworldly.

"What's our course status?" The AI remained silent. He rolled his eyes and shook his head. "Fine. Resume auto pilot."

"Confirmed. Re-establishing control of vehicle. Stand by."

"When you're done having a mini tantrum, can I get our course status?"

"We are off course by one hundred and twenty kilometers. Correcting to original path."

"Dismiss that. Is your threat assessment program off? That path was too dangerous. We need to find another route."

The display changed to a roadmap and multiple lines appeared along the trails ending at their destination. Two plausible routes lit up in blue.

"My threat assessment is sound. I calculated that the phenomenon would not likely occur again if we continued with our original plan. It is the fastest route."

"Well, you're wrong. Cuz that was deliberate."

"Explain."

"The Litigator is making this more difficult."

Another round of silence from the AI made him irritated. She was being childish.

"After calculating data from the weather anomaly, I have concluded that you are indeed correct. Starting new course."

The vehicle glided sideways and pivoted to the right at a thirty-degree angle. The map changed again to show they were on the first blue route that went in an arc around the area they had fled. Grannalt looked up at the sky.

Take that, you monster.

With the AI back in control, he undid the safety restraints and climbed to the back. Xander's breathing was not regulated and beads of sweat covered his forehead. He caught sight of a gash in the bodysuit on the side beneath the ribcage. Tiny nanobots squirmed like worker ants repairing the tissue in a deep wound. A closer observation found more wounds; some already being sealed up.

"What the hell kind of fight were you in?"

"Combat ratio was seven to one," the AI answered unexpectedly. "Although my charge was successful in bringing the conflict to an end, there was major damage to his body. The assailants had weapons capable of cutting his suit's material."

Grannalt touched the fabric, rubbing it between his thumb and forefinger. Reinforced combat material that could withstand bullets, laser fire, and knives. Only one kind of alloy had the ability to slice it which meant that group of humans had found someone who could manufacture it for their purpose. That angered him. Earth was devastated, yet there were humans who had no intention of changing their ways.

He caressed the kid's forehead and settled into the seat next to the medical unit. Xander reminded him of his children. A need to take care of him emerged. He had to make sure this child lived while he searched to save his own. Feeling hopeful, he reached out with his mind to the two he found. Sharp pain behind the back of his eyes was sent back from his son.

Rejected. Again.

Except this time Grannalt understood why. His children thought he needed protection.

"Don't underestimate my determination to protect you." He turned his head towards the front dash. "I need you to find some signatures for me. If they are along the route, I want to intercept."

"We are already behind schedule. I cannot take responsibility for a failed mission."

"For fuck's sake!" Grannalt took a deep breath. "I will take it. I swear…"

"The kill switch is not a valid option. You have threatened this yet have no intention of using it."

"You want to try me?"

The AI went silent again for a long period of time. Finally, she came back online.

"Please upload signatures. If they are on a similar course, we can veer off for no more than three hours."

"Good. I'll let you know when I establish another connection."

He sat back and let his eyes close.

Wait for me.

⤳

Xander woke up startled and tried to sit up only to have the tubes attached to him go taut, forcing him back down. A cluster of nanobots were finishing up repairs to his bodysuit, the wounds he sustained already dealt with.

"Patient has resumed consciousness. Detaching from apparatus. Health condition green."

The tubes went slack and one by one, their tiny tendrils slid from under his skin and retracted into the medical unit for sterilization. He was able to sit up and saw Grannalt sleeping across from him. In a panic, he scrambled to the front and hit the dash icon.

"Intruder alert! AI, why is there another person inside the vehicle?"

"Intrude alert not necessary. Person of concern is authorized user. Grannalt of Karysilan. He saved us from an assault by the Litigator."

Xander suddenly remembered seeing Grannalt through a fog of pain then slumped against the dash.

"Why would the Litigator attack us?"

"He doesn't want to talk to you yet." Grannalt had not moved or opened his eyes. "He's toying with you." Grannalt finally opened his eyes. "I'm betting there are others with the same idea."

"There are others who think they can destroy him and create a new world order."

Grannalt snorted.

"Yeah, I heard about that. Look," Grannalt leaned forward. "There's no reason for you to go about this alone. Your mother was probably hoping you would find a companion." He gestured to the inside of the vehicle. "This is a bit much for one person."

A thoughtful expression came over Xander. He had never asked for any details. Just went along with the plan. Now, he saw validity in what Grannalt was saying.

"If that's the case, then I hope you can fight. These people, these territories, I don't understand." He clutched his abdomen, wincing at the remembrance of pain. "What is happening?"

Grannalt smiled at him.

"Sometimes, it's best not to think about it."

He crawled up to the front and tapped the Analysis

icon on the display screen.

"Ready to send signatures."

Xander gave him a crazed stare as Grannalt took the electrodes that slithered from the dash and attached them to his temples.

"What signatures? For who?"

"My kids are in danger. I think they're close by."

Grannalt closed his eyes and concentrated.

A separate screen showed up on the dash. Waves on a graph fluctuated across it then transposed onto the roadmap of the adjacent screen. A third of the way up their route, the signatures blinked approximately twelve hundred miles off course to the left.

"Signatures established. Reiterating time limit of three hours to complete extraction."

"Understood." Grannalt opened his eyes and detached the electrodes. They went back into the dash. "Do you not condone this?" He asked Xander.

"Considering I barely came out of a huge fight alive, no. We have no idea what kind of danger," he put his fingers up in quotation marks, "your kids have gotten themselves into."

"But," Grannalt wagged a finger. "There are two of us."

"I have no idea how good you are at combat."

Grannalt's eyes grew bright and Xander pressed further against the dash.

"You'll know soon enough."

When Grannalt's eyes return to normal, Xander eased down into the seat next to him. He finally registered what the AI designated him as. Grannalt of Karysilan. The alien that the then United States of America had abducted from a crash site and used to jump start technology. And other horrors he didn't care to think about.

Yeah, he could fight. Probably better than me.

"ETA?"

"Detour will occur in thirty-two hours."

Xander scrolled through the travel data and stopped at one entry.

"What does that mean?" He pointed at it. "There is no indication of being on land."

Grannalt smirked at him, a mischievous grin spreading.

"Didn't you know? This thing can fly."

Xander's eyes went wide and his mouth gaped open. Grannalt started laughing. He switched screens and went through the settings. There it was in bold letters in the menu.

"Then why are we wasting time driving?" He exploded. "We could cover way more distance in the air."

Grannalt stopped laughing and gave him a stern look.

"Because it's dangerous. Do you see anything else flying around? Know why? If there was any inkling that air travel was possible, people would lose their minds. This vehicle would be taken from you in a heartbeat as you lay dead in the dirt."

Xander reared back from the verbal assault.

"The New Order surely has them," he mumbled.

"Yeah, and they also know better than to show it."

Exhaustion hit him like a brick, making his body go limp. He struggled to stay upright. Grannalt leaned over and gently pushed his head down against the window.

"You got up way to quick. Take it easy. We'll talk later."

Xander tried to voice protest, but nothing came out. Instead, his eyes fluttered close.

Chapter Three

HOW ABOUT A SAVIOR?

The next shelter the siblings came across was on the edge of the continent. Dark sand covered the beach and the ocean water barely came up to the shoreline. Every building in the compound had been damaged from what looked like airstrikes. There wasn't much to salvage, and he didn't trust the structure integrity of the only building still standing. Seth could sense his pursuers closing in.

"What do you want to do?" Erin asked.

She looked around the area, her expression dubious.

"We need to cross that." He pointed to the ocean.

"Oh." Erin's eyes went wide as her mouth formed the word. "This place has to have a bunker or hangar with vehicles in it."

Seth nodded and headed towards one of the dilapidated buildings. Its shape was similar to the battle stations he had seen when the two were initially on the run. Erin followed and they both went through it searching for the panel that would open the lower level bays. After nearly two hours, Erin shouted.

"Found it!"

She typed in a range of codes she remembered before the war into the flat keypad on the panel. On the fifth one, the panel glowed, and an entrance revealed itself.

The motion lights came on, though most of them were damaged, making the area dim. Large pieces of debris were atop the vehicles in the bay. They looked up and saw the ceiling had caved in. A vehicle near the hangar doors was not buried like the others. Seth went over to it and pushed the slab of ceiling off the hood. Erin manipulated the doors until they sprung open.

"This one is for traveling on water." Erin ran her fingers across the designation plaque. "Lucky, huh?"

"Makes sense considering where this base is located."

Erin backed out of the vehicle and started feeling along the hangar walls. At one section, the wall receded and a row of one-inch cylinders appeared. She squealed as she grabbed one and ran back to the vehicle.

"I've got the key!"

"A key," Seth corrected her.

She pursed her lips and frowned at him. Then she inserted the cylinder in the initiation panel. The control console lit up and the soft hum of power came to their ears.

"Please input DNA signatures for start-up sequence. Or scan iris and fingerprints."

The AI voice was male with a slight tenor. A tray flipped out and laid flat against the small screen on the right. Seth leaned over and let the system map his irises while he placed his right hand on the platform below that began scanning.

"Analysis complete. Please advise copilot to input DNA signature or scan iris and fingerprints."

Erin did the same and giggled when she was done.

"That was interesting," she laughed.

"Operators verified. Initiating start up sequence. GPS system online."

Erin clapped her hands then strapped into the passenger side. Seth settled in the driver side and found his straps to connect. Once they clicked in place, he tapped the main screen. The tray receded into the dash. He found the icon to open the hangar and tapped it. Alarms went off, their sound warped from damage. The hangar struggled to open, making a loud grinding noise as the doors slid to either side. Late afternoon light flooded into the bay.

From the map he determined their coordinates and used the touch screen to enter them.

"Current start designation: Ocean Beach California. Destination Queensland Australia. Approximate mileage seven thousand five hundred miles. Please specify speed."

"Are we going straight across?" Erin asked.

Seth stared out at the horizon and thought about it for a moment. They were being chased but he also knew neither could go too fast or too high in case they were spotted by a hostile territory group. Even on water both parties may not be safe.

"Three hundred miles per hour, with plus or minus fifty increase."

"Calculating." The navigation map rotated and changed, zooming in on the path it had created. "Estimated time of arrival, thirty-six hours. If this is satisfactory, please touch the Accept icon."

Seth used his index finger to do as instructed then hit the start icon. The vehicle's engines came to life and hovered off the ground.

"Route verified. Starting navigation."

It eased itself through the open hangar towards the open waters. Once it reached the edge of the shoreline, it shot out gaining speed until it reached the suggested max at three hundred and twenty-five.

Erin let out a rejoicing yell and drummed her hands on the dash. They were on their way to another part of the planet they had never been.

With the vehicle in autopilot, the two siblings roamed the cabin. Behind the front seats was open space. Along the walls were benches and storage bins. Erin rummaged through a few of them and found supplies for diving next to weapons. On the other side, Seth found the rations bin. A panel on the wall nearby had a picture of a table. He touched it and a dark square formed in the center of the space. It recessed then rose up two and a half feet.

"Ooh!" Erin slid onto the bench across from him and laid her hands on the table. "We get to do some fine dining."

Seth grabbed two trays from the bin, added bottled water and tossed them in the microwave for one minute as instructed on the package. He found the utensils bin and pulled out two forks. When the microwave beeped indicating it was done, he dragged the trays out slowly due to their heat and set them on the table. He sat on the bench.

"Bon Appetit," he said softly.

Erin tore off the rest of the seal and stared at the meal inside.

"Pork chops?" She pointed to the side dish. "Rice maybe?"

"Just eat it." Seth removed the seal on his and took a bite. "Could be chicken."

They ate in silence. When they were done, the trays went onto the incinerator and Seth lowered the table. Another icon on the wall showed bunk beds. Hitting that activated the benches on the wall to extend out while a second row appeared above them. Erin ran over to the storage bins on her side and came across a wide one labeled bedding. She reached in and extracted two pillows.

"Ta-da!"

She tossed him one.

"We should get some real rest while we can."

"Good idea."

Erin climbed up to the bunk bed above Seth. She raised the pillow over her head and placed it underneath. Seth tucked his behind his head as well. Before either knew it, they were fast asleep, exhaustion finally caught up with them.

A sharp nudge in his head woke Seth from a deep sleep. He sat up wincing as it turned to pain. He grabbed the left side of face, pressing hard to alleviate it. Realizing what it was, he immediately cut off the intruder. Their mother was again trying to find them. Being caught off guard meant the attempt probably succeeded. Seth frowned in frustration as the pain ebbed away.

"That hurt," Erin piped up as she sat up in her bunk.

Seth looked over at the counter embedded in the opposite wall. They had only slept six hours. His body wasn't complaining. Constant uninterrupted sleep felt like an eternity. He searched his mind and concluded their mother had figured out their coordinates.

"There's that," he sighed.

For the duration of their trip, the two siblings took it easy. They went over the map, used the sonar to scan the depths of the ocean, but mostly rested. Five hours from the destination on the mainland, the vehicle lurched and its speed decreased.

"Warning. System malfunction."

Seth scrambled out of his bunk and went to the dash. "Diagnosis?"

"Couplings overheated. Stabilization module damaged."

"Why didn't you tell us that before?" Erin snapped.

The AI seemed to pause as if insulted.

"Initial scan was completed. Systems showed green."

"Can it be corrected?"

"Negative. Sped decreased to cool down."

"How long do you have?"

Seth asked in a concerned tone. The AI picked it up.

"ETA to landfall three hours. New destination, designated Brisbane. Please remove the core key before exiting the vehicle."

Seth nodded.

"Noted. As long as we get to solid ground, we'll be grateful. Thank you."

Erin's face scrunched up with sadness.

"We're going to have to go on foot again."

"Yeah."

Forty minutes after entering what used to be Brisbane, the vehicle stalled out in midair and dropped to the ground smoldering. The frame creaked as it warped from the impact and heat. The doors opened and Seth removed the key, handing it over to Erin. She palmed it for a while before sticking it in one of her pockets. Seth stared at the massive assault rifles sitting on the racks inside the storage wall. If there had been any handguns, he would have taken one or two. They replenished their packs before donning them and left the vehicle. Above them, the sky was a swirl of orange, pink, and lavender. The beginnings of sunset.

This is bad.

Seth watched the cloud of dust ahead get bigger as it closed in on him and his sister. They had been walking for hours and there was no sign of shelter for miles. Night had turned into day and the sun had only just peeked out to shed some light. With nowhere to run that meant they would have to stand their ground right then.

He took a deep breath and felt his sister position herself beside him. As a modified vehicle came into view, he saw at least six people hanging out of its windows, yelling while banging weapons against the frame.

Both siblings were trained in combat. He was certain they could hold their own with four or five assailants. More than that posed a problem. From what he could make out, there were more inside the vehicle in addition to the six.

"What are we going to do?" Erin asked. Her voice was tense with anxiety.

"Steady," he told her. "Don't panic."

Before the vehicle came to a complete stop, four men jumped out and ran towards them like a horde of banshees. They all wore face paint, leather garments and kill trophies around their necks. One had a small skull hanging from thin rope. Seth nearly gagged. Erin clamped a hand over her mouth in horror then removed it.

"Why? What kind of monsters are these people?"

"The worst kind," he replied.

The four converged on them. They kept close together making sure the enemy didn't come between them. Erin grabbed hold of the first one nearest to her by the neck, surprising them. Forming her other hand into a spade, she punched through the thin leather shirt. She felt the resistance as her fingers enter flesh, becoming wet and gummy. Pulling out her hand, Erin immediately pivoted towards the second assailant.

The enemy dodged her advance, but she weaved back around and hit them in the back side where their kidney would be. They winced faltering for a bit then recovered. She leapt in the air and came down with her fist aimed at the top of their head. They managed to tilt their head away only to be hit in the side of the head, going down.

Seth was evading the two on him, not letting either land a blow. The two became infuriated and decided to come at him together. He gave a small grin. That's what he wanted. Right as they came in front of him, side by side ready to plow him into the ground, he ducked down and turned sideways. He fell between them, grabbing hold of both their heads and smashed them together with as much force as he could. They went to their knees, shook their heads and got ready to stand.

A blast hit directly in front of the siblings and their enemy, knocking all of them back twenty feet. Two of the enemy fighters were lying face down, limbs blown off. The other two scrambled to their feet and went for the Seth and Erin. The vehicle stopped and the rest of the passengers spilled out. Seth counted six in total.

So, there were ten of these bastards.

A man and woman strolled towards them while the two enemy fighters dragged the siblings by their hair to meet them.

"What we got here?" The woman was tall. Her skin was coated in a bronze paint and her eyes were defined by the black strip of paint across them. "Couple of kids roaming the Earth all by their lonesome?" A metal head-dress sat atop her head covering most of her blonde hair. "Whatcha' think?" She turned to her counterpart.

The man spit onto the ground and looked down on them with disgust. He also wore a metal piece on his head though smaller. His blue eyes were menacing amid the face paint.

"Kids? Nah. The way that little cunt stuck her fingers in our guy, that's no kid."

He walked to Erin and kicked her hard in the abdomen, knocking the air out of her. She couldn't even yell or cry. Only a high-pitched wheeze came out as she double over in the fetal position. Seth felt his body instinctively struggle to get to her before he thought better and stopped.

Too late.

The woman was before him in a blink of the eye, her fist slamming into his face. He tasted blood.

"I agree. Kids should know better than to try and fight when they're outmatched.

"Whoa! Take a look at their gear," one of the other fighters cried out.

Two of the enemy had found their packs and were rummaging through them. Seth cursed silently. Their belongings were strewn all over.

"Well, look it that. We got ourselves a little score." The man laughed. "Grab the shit. We're gonna' have some fun before we go." He pulled out a serrated blade and knelt by Erin. "You want first go?" He turned to his female counterpart.

"Oh, yeah." She addressed the two closest to Seth. "You can start on that one. Make sure to get all the good organs when you're down plowing that sweet ass." She turned her attention back to Erin and took the blade from her partner. "I'm gonna make you scream like you've never had in your life."

She grabbed hold of Erin's tunic and tried to saw through the fabric. The edges slid across the material barely shredding it.

"What the hell?" The woman yelled, punching Erin in frustration with the hilt.

Seth tried to get loose of his enemies' grip. One of the men stomped on his chest, making him lay flat on the ground. He felt a small snap in his ribcage.

"Don't worry about them. She'll get that shit off soon enough." They pulled out a different kind of sharp weapon made from a dull silver alloy and Seth knew it could cut his clothes. "You should get it all out of your system while you can. When we start slicing you up for dinner, it's best you have nothing left to fight for."

Seeing the solution to her problem, the female leader pulled out the same kind of weapon and smiled down at the sister. She licked her lips in anticipation. Seth heard the sound of his sister's tunic ripping as he was held down, his enemy poised over him with the cutting tool positioned at his crotch.

"You won't be needing that thing anymore. We can start there," he sneered, a manic look in his eyes like that of hunter ready to devour its prey.

Then he was gone.

Or rather, the entire top part of his body had disappeared. Seth looked behind him and saw one of the other fighters holding him down had no arms above the biceps. In a delayed reaction, the man began to scream, falling backwards. The two leaders were hunkered down on the ground, the top of the female's headdress burning red hot.

Coming up from the right alongside the enemy vehicle was a much larger one with its weapons system activated. The blue glow of the cannon iris glared at them. Seth knew it had to be the two aliens they had robbed. The giant hovercraft slowed to a stop over five hundred yards from them and Fravral climbed out. Up close, the alien was way taller than expected. Seth felt trepidation. Even if the two enemy factions fought, the attention would revert to them.

"This ain't your party," the male leader spat. "You're gonna pay for what you done to my boys."

"My business is with those two. When I get back what is mine, you can continue on with whatever you were doing."

"Nah." The male leader stood. "That ain't how this works."

"Is that right?"

From the pod attached to the back of the ship, black

tendrils snaked out into the air and whipped around as the cybok emerged. His massive frame stepped out, black on black eyes peering at the enemy. The leaders hesitated for a split second.

Consumed by anger, the female leader charged first. Seth watched in awe as the big alien guy punched her so hard she flew back past them, landing with a thud. He was sure every bone in her body was broken. Her eyes were still open, tongue hanging out the side of her mouth like out of a cartoon. He could see where her skull had caved in on impact.

The remaining fighters gathered their courage and went for the cybok.

"No!" The male leader got to his feet, still stunned by the death of his partner. "Stop!"

The cybok's hands receded into their wrists and the arms configured into glowing cannons. Their power indicators went up two notches, leaving the other four dark. Two rounds were released simultaneously. The first hit the farthest fighter in the charge, obliterating everything except the legs below the calves, a hand and a sliver of the head. The other hit the enemy vehicle, sending it into the air. It landed still intact but smoking. Explosions erupted from the engine.

One of the fighters changed course and went for the big alien guy. He got right on him and delivered a direct blow to the head. The alien guy didn't budge, instead, grabbing the fighter by the neck and lifting him inches off the ground. He caught a glimpse of the small skull on the rope necklace and fingered it before letting it slip away. Something awful glinted in his eyes as they locked with the enemy fighter.

"Did you do this?" Fravral asked.

The fighter grinned proudly.

"I got the privilege to help. The bossman knows how

to make quick work of the tender meat. Got to keep the token, though."

The man was able to get a short cackle out before the alien guy crushed his neck, severing the head. It lopped sideways then fell off, the rest of his body sliding down from lack of grip. The alien guy's attention fell on the male leader who was already on his feet, serrated blade held up in a strike position.

"I've changed my mind," Fravral said. "You humans don't deserve to live."

While the cybok went to dispatch the rest of the fighters, Fravral and the leader charged each other. Seth was able to raise his head enough to see the clash. He thought he saw air being sliced. Confirmation came as the male leader's body, still in a charging stance began to peel apart vertically. The alien guy stepped away to avoid the blood splatter that started.

Seth was about to roll over when darkness fell before him. He had not seen the cybok move towards him. He stared into two pools of black as the creature hovered over him. He could hear his sister screaming in pain while Fravral demanded answers.

"Where is it? You little runt," he called out to Seth. "I'll make her feel a lot more pain than this if you don't give back what you took from me." To the Cybok, he said, "Tear him apart if you have to. Find it."

The creature leaned over him, his arms back to normal. With one hand, the creature tore open his tunic and pressed into his chest. Seth coughed up blood and winced. The cybok halted.

They locked eyes.

Am I imagining things? Seth focused on the Cybok.

Deep in the abyss of the Cybok's eyes was a longing. The hand on his chest reached up and caressed his hair. His head tilted to one side as if examining him.

"What are you doing?" Fravral yelled.

To Seth's surprise, the Cybok fondled his entire body before pulling out the thing in his pocket. Then the creature sniffed him from bottom to top. As he moved away, Seth could see his sister.

"Get away from him!" Fravral dropped Erin and headed towards the Cybok. "What is wrong with you?" He saw the module in the Cybok's hand. "You have it. Good. Let's go."

Fravral walked off. When the Cybok didn't follow, he stopped and turned back with a confused expression. Then he let out a sigh.

"Fine. I won't leave them here to die. Pick them up. We're leaving."

Not being gentle in the slightest, the Cybok took Seth by the wrist, dragged him over to his sister and did her the same. He flung them over his shoulders as they gasped in pain and headed to the ship. Seth caught a glimpse of Fravral.

He was not happy.

Grannalt was leaned close to the dash after the display showed the scene unfolding a good ten kilometers ahead at the signatures' location. The two had been moving at a constant speed for a day and a half then stopped before resuming at a snail's pace. The AI refused to recalculate to accommodate the change and Grannalt began to panic. He saw the swells of dust earlier as they approach the area and had the AI zoom in. His organs pounded in his chest as he watched helplessly while the group of thugs had fun. When the hovercraft showed up out of nowhere from the other side and the Cybok came out, he slammed a fist on the dash.

"Go faster!" He demanded.

"Vehicle currently at optimal speed for the situation following assessment. Acceleration would not curb the situation," the AI replied calmly.

"She's right. Getting there a second or two quicker would do nothing." Xander set one foot on the dash and sat back.

Grannalt undid his safety straps as the vehicle approached the combat zone. He saw his children being hauled off like sacks towards the hovercraft.

"Open the doors!"

The vehicle stopped fifty yards from Fravral and the Cybok and Grannalt got out. He went to the front of the vehicle and reaching by his sides, pulled out two short metal cylinders. As he held them up in a combat stance, they extended from both ends. Now holding two long metal staffs, Grannalt stared down the two Relliants.

"Give me back my children." His voice was steady, dripping with rage.

Fravral stopped walking and turned to him. The soft hum from the two staffs vibrating with energy arrived in his ears and he frowned. The Cybok also halted.

"These are yours?"

Grannalt swung the staffs one hundred and eighty degrees and crouched, ready to launch. Fravral held up a hand.

"They stole my locator from me. You, most of all, know how important it is."

"So what? They're barely out of infancy. That's what I despise about your race."

Fravral gave him a stern look.

"Are you really prepared to fight me and a Cybok with only those weapons?"

"Not without help." Xander said as he emerged from the vehicle.

"Give…them…back!" Grannalt demanded fervently.

Fravral seemed to relent. He turned to the Cybok. "Drop 'em."

The Cybok set Erin on the ground. Grannalt relaxed his stance and stood while Xander picked her up and headed back to the vehicle. When the creature didn't release his son, Grannalt tensed up. Fravral turned to the Cybok.

"What are you doing? I said let him go."

Grannalt searched the Cybok's face for intent and saw…loneliness. The Cybok tightened its grip on Seth. From the corner of his eye, Grannalt could tell Fravral noticed it as well.

"I understand what you feel," Grannalt said to the Cybok. "But you can't have him. He's too young to be with a species like you." The Cybok stepped back. "Please. He's my child."

The Cybok reluctantly walked towards Grannalt then laid Seth down before backing away. Xander retrieved him and got him in the back of the vehicle. Grannalt let the staffs recede back into their housing units.

"You should have known better," he said to Fravral. "Having those Cyboks created together meant they were eternally bonded. The least you could have done was put him out of his misery and save such pain."

"If I were you, I'd get him far away. I doubt my Cybok will let him go so easily." Fravral walked to his ship. To the Cybok, he called out. "Let's go. Commander Gragor is waiting."

With one last look of longing for Seth, the Cybok followed Fravral. When the hovercraft took off, Grannalt exhaled hard from relief. He felt his body start to shake. If a fight had occurred, he knew Xander and himself would be dead and possibly his children. Xander came back out of the vehicle and began gathering up the scattered supplies.

"Well, I gotta' say, they are well trained. These provisions are top notch. The backpacks too. Survival techniques, minus this incident, are good."

Grannalt simply nodded and helped him with the task at hand.

Back in the vehicle, Grannalt sat in the back with his children. The AI for the medical unit was running an analysis. Xander hopped in the front and the hatch doors closed. The vehicle AI came online.

"Retrieval commenced within time limit. Still on schedule. Resuming course for Litigator location."

The vehicle spun around and headed back towards the main road. Grannalt stroked both his children's foreheads. Erin opened her eyes and stared at her for a moment.

"At least we have the same eyes," she whispered in what sounded like disappointment.

She slipped back unconscious. Grannalt let a tiny smile form. A thought invaded his mind.

So reckless.

He looked over at his son, falling deep into an abyss of sleep.

That's no way to say thank you to your mother.

There was something like a sigh.

Fine. Thank you. Nice to meet you. Mother.

Grannalt clamped a hand over his mouth to stop the cry ready to escape. Tears of happiness streaked down his face.

⌒

All the exterior cameras near the upper level of the facility trained on the small group of refugees huddled on the platform. They were wearing tattered cloaks caked with weeks of debris from being in the elements. Professor Bartley sat sideways at his desk staring at the six holoscreens, three in a row, as he assessed the area.

He scanned each person, trying to get a good look at their faces. He found those with any decent length of hair had forgone grooming long ago, the others having shaved it all off. Hungry, tired, desperate. Yet something was very wrong about their demeanor.

"Professor," a man's voice crackled through the commlink.

"What you got?" He swiveled in his chair so that he sat facing the screens.

"I spotted something on the outer perimeter."

The screen on the bottom far left panned out and zoomed in a few splotches among the petrified trees twisted from the super-heated blasts during the battle. As still as the blobs of white were, he could tell they were people. The white uniforms gave them away. The New Order.

That's what was wrong. Some of the refugees were frightened. Like they had been coerced into asking for asylum. Professor Bartley frowned. He knew what that meant. A closer look at the rest of the area showed him how much fire power the New Order had brought with them. Two laser cannons, a plasma launcher, and assault rifles in the hands of operatives from every angle trained on the platform.

"I think this may be a trap, sir," the man said back.

"Oh, I'm sure it is."

"How should we explain denied access?"

"We're not."

There was a long pause. Right as the commlink crackled again, Vasence appeared on the screen to his right with a face contorted in anger and flushed pink.

"Are you mad?" He yelled. "We can't just let those New Order assholes infiltrate us!"

"Who says they're getting in?" He tapped the commlink. "Open the hangar."

Professor Bartley got up from his chair and headed out of his chamber wearing only a pair of drawstring pants and an open shirt.

"I'm coming down."

Vasence stiffened and the sentry outside remained eerily silent.

The New Order scout adjusted the lens on his vision goggles and zeroed in on the platform. He saw the top half of the facility begin to raise and he smiled. Turning to the other two members beside him, he nodded.

"Looks like they took the bait. Easy access."

The one farthest from him leaned back and sat on his knees.

"This only works because of the state this planet is in. After we reestablish order, all this will be on lock down, for sure."

"Of course," the scout answered. "Get ready for my signal," he ordered through the commlink. "The moment our people are in range of the threshold, we give weapon support."

A round of confirmations from the section leaders came through. The hangar was halfway open.

On the platform, the six New Order operatives sitting amongst the seventy refugees kept their heads down while they readied their weapons hidden beneath their cloaks. One of the refugees let out an anguished breath.

The operative close to him nudged his gun in their side and whispered, "Keep quiet."

From the hangar came four groups of five guards wearing black full body combat suits. Two of the units were fully armed which surprised the operatives on the platform. They were under the impression that most of the people in the facility had talents or were merely civilians, meaning no need for actual weapons. The leader of the first group came up to them.

"Please follow us in an orderly fashion as quickly as you can to the entrance. Once inside, you will be scanned per our quarantine procedure."

Everyone cautiously arose and kept close while moving as instructed. The New Order leader within the refugee line noted the sparse amount of guards near the five hundred foot threshold up ahead before the entrance began. In another two minutes, his men would be in range.

Laser fire came streaking across the sky from behind the facility, targeting the cannons on the hillside. The New Order operatives stared up in awe then fear as rounds rained down on them. One of the cannon operators managed to activate the shield and protect both the weapon and his men. The other cannon was hit but still capable of firing.

The operatives on the platform pushed away from the refugees and began firing onto the facility workers. A melee of crossfire ensued. The facility group closest to the entrance moved forward and ushered the true refugees towards the entrance. Some of the refugees were hit and others helped them along, dragging them when deemed necessary.

Klaxons went off at the back of the entrance along with flashing lights as a corridor appeared from within. The AI's voice boomed out into the open air.

"Warning! Inner sector unlocked. Facility host not secured."

The New Order operatives watched facility guards nearby turn their heads towards the sound, their faces horror stricken. They immediately moved out of the way, leaving the operatives in a cluster of confusion.

Professor Bartley emerged from the hangar taking long strides. The warning lights flickered off his bare skin as he passed the threshold. His hair whipped in the heated air from the laser fire. He pulled off his shirt and with each thunderous step, began to transform. The dark spot along his spine grew darker and leathery wings sprouted, spanning out three feet. They got bigger, wider as he leapt into the air at lightning speed. The wings became translucent, the joints a rusty red that sparkled in the daylight. He dove right into the shield, cracking it open like an eggshell as he plowed into the cannon, destroying it.

The operatives inside fired on him. His wings flapped shut and the rounds bounced off, not leaving a mark. When they stopped for a split second, pondering their next move, Professor Bartley finished them off. His wings opened and long tendrils with sharp ends shot out from each side of him, piercing the first row of operatives. He flapped his wings forward. The force dragged the impaled men off the hill and into the air where he retracted the tendrils. The men's screams faded in the distance as they fell to their deaths.

The second cannon fired. Professor Bartley veered to the right in time to avoid the blast. Another volley came as he corrected his position in the air. He closed his wings to absorb the impact and it knocked him into the side of the cliff.

His wings opened. Amber eyes, full of rage, glowed. A high pitch scream erupted from his mouth, causing everyone in the surrounding area to fall to the ground covering their ears. The translucent parts of his wings turned dark pink.

"What the fuck is that?" The lead operative on the platform screamed as he tried to retreat with the survivors of his unit.

The lead scout managed to rise from the ground, ears bleeding, and target Professor Bartley with the cannon.

To his amazement, he and the Professor locked eyes. "Oh shit!"

"Shoot it down!" His commanding officer yelled.

Before he could get out of range after launching the blast, Professor Bartley shot forth, decimating the hillside, the blast ricocheting off his wings as the cannon broke apart.

Inside the facility, everyone stared up at the nearest holoscreen showing the battle outside and marveled at Professor Bartley's form. Vasence and Lillian stood side by side in his lab.

"Did you know?" She asked.

Vasence slowly shook his head.

"If I had, there's no way I would have engaged with him like I have."

"I've never seen anything like it."

"Oh, I have. Once."

"And?" Lillian's brow raised.

Vasence turned to her, eyes wide with trepidation.

"I think we need to be more cautious with him."

"What about those New Order soldiers outside?"

"They don't have a chance in hell." He walked over to his desk. "Come on. We need to extract some information from the fallen."

"Extract?"

Lillian saw the hideous look on his face and didn't bother to wait for clarification. She immediately understood what he meant.

THE MORE THE MERRIER

Arctic air formed frost on the front view shield of the Relliant combat ship as it sped across the mountainous terrain. Fravral had made it back to the ship in record time, the Cybok not leaving his pod in an act of protest. The thing wouldn't even speak to him.

Stubborn creature!

The way it sounded in his head made him snap into attention. Relliants had always referred to Cyboks as creatures, yet the League and other races did not. To his race, they were merely weapons for war. A feeling of self-loathing and regret came over him. Grannalt's words repeated in his head. The two Cyboks had been inseparable and the Karysilan was right. When one died, the other was left to languish.

"I am truly sorry," he said, knowing the Cybok couldn't hear him.

He hit the button to clear the front screen of frost and glanced over at the navigation display that showed Gragor's location. He squinted at the blip then looked up towards the signal. Up ahead was a mountain somehow still intact, its newly formed icy snowcaps glistening a pastel orange from the sunlight.

"What the hell are you doing way up there?"

Fravral searched for any sign of the commander's

ship and found wreckage at the mountain base. He zoomed in for a closer inspection. From the looks of it, there was no way to fix it. The insignia was not Gragor's but Bree's. A glint of hope crossed his face. The blackened husk of a wrecked vehicle from an explosion sat farther away. Movement from a cave opening near the top caught his eye and he saw a figure standing in its center. Commander Gragor pointed down, a request for him to land by Bree's wreckage.

I finally found you.

Fravral breathed a sigh of relief. He maneuvered his ship to land next to Bree's and saw multiple life signatures pop up on his screen.

That's odd.

After shutting down the engines, he opened the ramp and stepped outside. The arctic air was still present even at such low levels of the mountain although there was a balminess. From the other ship, Bree came down the opened ramp. Fravral was about to embrace him then saw his eyes. Something cold and unmoving lay deep in them. The Command Fleet officer was always a quiet storm, but this was different. It made his skin crawl.

"Commander Fravral," Bree greeted him from a few feet away.

"Captain. It's good to see you again."

"What took you so long? We were tracking your movements and you seemed to be having fun trekking all over the terrain."

From behind Fravral, Gragor slapped a hand on his shoulder.

"Yes. What were you doing?"

"Slight snag. Some human children got hold of the locator and we had to give chase." He pointed to his ship. "Got it back though." He looked around. "Is Captain Craig not with you? Did you get separated during the battle?"

He saw Bree's facial expression go blank, his eyes dead. Gragor seemed to tense. Fravral realized the reason immediately. Before he could say anything, Gragor patted his shoulder and walked around him to the ship. Bree's mouth opened. Nothing came out.

"Craig has returned to the stars in spirit. He is gone," Bree finally replied before turning away and headed into his ship. "Come. We have things to do."

Fravral kept himself from expressing the shock he felt and followed the two officers. He was taken aback by the humans being housed inside the hangar. They were tethered to the grates on the floor and angry. One of them tried to stare him down. Fravral tilted his head and gave him a sinister smile. The man flinched and turned away.

"What's this about?"

Fravral waved an arm before him.

Gragor knelt by the one who glared at him.

"Have you not heard about the New Order that converged on the scene some years ago?" He asked Fravral.

"Oh, I heard. It's the most ridiculous things humans have done yet."

"Then you know of their other agenda?"

Fravral frowned. *That was bad enough, wasn't it?* Gragor saw his confusion.

"They want to eliminate the Litigator. He's a main obstacle in their plans for restructure."

A burst of laughter came out of Fravral to his own surprise. He stopped himself and stared at the humans huddled on the floor.

"Are you serious? Have they gone mad?" He addressed the humans. "Have you?" He was given more angry stares for an answer. "So, what are we doing?"

Gragor stood and paced the hangar while Bree remained rooted in place by the console.

"I didn't have my soldiers mutiny for the sake of Earth only to have the Litigator wipe out the planet as an afterthought."

"Does this mean we are on a mission?"

"Will you continue to accompany us if so?"

Fravral contemplated the pros and cons of the situation. On one hand, they were probably the best race to negotiate with the thing. On the other, they could be annihilated on a whim if the Litigator saw fit. He looked at the pitiful humans whose goals were laughable at best, yet he knew they had every intention of going forward with their plans.

He exhaled slowly. "I am at your command." He gave Gragor the Relliant salute.

"Good. We're going to need a ride."

"I figured as much. Your ship is beyond help," he said to Bree. To both of them he asked. "What's the deal with these humans?"

Bree's eyes turned bright and deadly.

"Oh, we haven't decided yet."

"Do they still have communicators?"

Gragor tossed him one.

"Turned off. Tracking disabled.

"I say we leave them here and let their leaders come retrieve them." Fravral saw the frown on Gragor's face. He understood why. "If we get them far enough away from here then drop them in the next territory, that should suffice."

The humans went pale with fear. From what he could see, they were only equipped with minimal protective gear since their vehicle was out of commission. Their survival depended on the weather and how long it would take for search and rescue.

"You tout about saving humans yet you're willing to let us die like animals in the elements!" One of the humans leaned forward, red faced with rage, the tether stopping them from going any further. "We never asked for your help in the first place!"

Bree took one step towards the human and knocked them out with a sweeping kick. The human's head snapped back as their body slumped against the person next to them. His eyes grew brighter with hostility.

"We saved humans because it was the right thing to do. Your actions negate the wishes of every soul lost. Bow in shame."

The rest of the humans went silent as they stared up at Bree. His malcontent permeated the hangar. Fravral nodded in agreement. He backed away from Bree. There was so much malice, it even frightened him. Gragor appeared to feel the same.

The three of them got the humans on his small ship, packing them in like sardines, and Fravral settled in the cockpit. Gragor glanced back at the smaller pod attached to the back end. His brows went up.

"Commander Fravral, what's in the pod?"

"My Cybok. He's angry at me and won't come out."

Gragor's eyes nearly bulged out of their sockets.

"You have a Cybok with you?" His voice was an octave higher than normal. Then he frowned. "Didn't you have two?"

Fravral tensed at the command console.

"The other used himself as a shield to save the two of us."

"So, now you have a rogue Cybok with an abandonment complex." Bree said it so nonchalant that Fravral wasn't sure if he was being mean or sympathetic. "When does he come out?"

"Oh, when we have to dispatch crazy humans out hunting their own kind for food and murder."

Bree finished securing the humans then sat at the secondary navigation screen. Gragor sat in the copilot seat next to Fravral.

"And another thing. I ran into the parent of those children I chased. He's a Karysilan traveling along with one of those bioengineered humans in a utility vehicle."

Gragor seemed intrigued.

"Is that so? Maybe we'll run into them again."

"I hope not," Fravral snapped.

"Why is that?"

"My Cybok." Fravral took a deep breath. "He seems to have an attachment to the boy."

Bree gave him a knowing side glance. Gragor shook his head.

"Well, that's unfortunate. All the same. I would like to have chat with the Karysilan."

Last checks complete, Fravral initiated the engines and waited for the craft to hover ten feet off the ground before hitting the thrusters. The territory up ahead started gathering storm clouds and he wondered if it was a natural occurrence.

On the outskirts, in the middle of a small windstorm, the humans were untethered and released with one of their communicators back online. Gragor tossed it amongst them and headed back into the ship.

"Monsters!" One of the humans yelled over the wind.

"Leaving us out here to die is no different than murder," another added.

Gragor stopped at the opened ramp.

"If you die from this tiny windstorm, then you deserved it."

As he entered the cockpit, the wind seemed to shift. A brutal blast swept across the terrain, scattering the humans in different directions. One of the humans grabbed hold of the communicator and held onto it for dear life. He could hear their cries while the ramp closed to seal the Relliants in. Gragor looked up at the sky. The wind suddenly subsided.

What games are you playing? He asked the Litigator.

⸺

Faint beeps woke Seth from his pained slumber. His face was slightly sore, and his abdomen felt tight. Then he remembered his ribs being broken and his jaw having a possible hairline fracture.

"Repairs complete. Disengaging probes."

He forced his eyes open and watched the tiny thread-like tubes slither out of him. The grogginess lingered making him slow to sit up. Mild sedative. His injuries weren't severe enough to put him out in a deep sleep. Next to him, his sister was leaning sideways against the seat facing him. He was certain her injuries were worse than his yet she was no longer hooked to the med unit.

She must have been watching me sleep.

He reached over and stroked the top of her head. Movement from the other side caught his attention and Grannalt came in view. They shared a silent moment until it was broken by Xander calling to them.

"I think we may have to stop for a while. Seems the Litigator is having another tantrum in another territory."

"The Litigator?" Seth asked.

"Do you not know about that species?" Grannalt replied.

"I have heard of them. Evolved from carnivores. Is he really the one manipulating the weather in the territories?"

"Not entirely. He just likes to deter others from getting to him."

"Oh. Then, he's a menace."

Xander laughed followed by Grannalt.

Seth took stock of the inside of the vehicle for the first time and was impressed. He saw the haul of supplies his sister and he had compiled in a see-through containment near the back. Relief consumed him. His sister was safe from the elements and could relax a bit. It didn't surprise him how easily she had fallen asleep.

"So can you," Grannalt said.

"I know. She takes priority in my mind."

"That's good. I'm glad the two of you are together."

There was a sadness in Grannalt's tone and Seth understood why. Three other siblings were unaccounted for. As far as he could tell, two of them were not on the planet. He had no idea if they were evacuated during the battle or dead. The other had blocked his communication completely. Erin stirred awake and stretched her body out while letting out a loud and obnoxious yawn. She rotated her neck, each move creating small cracking sounds.

"Wow, I must have been tired."

"That was a little overdramatic," Seth whispered.

"Hmm?"

Then she turned to Grannalt and bear hugged him, putting both their bodies in awkward positions on the seat. Grannalt had to return the gesture enable to stay upright. Erin giggled.

"Founjya'!" The joy on her face was priceless.

"What would you prefer we call you?" Seth asked. "It seems weird to call you by your name but calling you mother is, well…"

"I," Grannalt hesitated. "Whichever you think is best."

"I'm calling you Mom," Erin stated.

Seth hung his head in defeat. He was not going to argue with her. There was no point. He settled correctly in the seat and let his head fall back on the neck cushion.

Taking a few deep breaths, he raised his head and looked at Xander.

"We're going to see the Litigator?"

"Yes."

"For what reason? As long as he's not killing anyone, what's the rush?"

"Because that is exactly his plan. To wipe out the planet and start over."

Seth pursed his lips. He could see the logic but at the same time felt it unnecessary. The typography display showed a storm brewing then dissipate.

That's not natural at all.

He wondered what any of them could possibly say to persuade such a creature. Erin released Grannalt and scooted to the edge of the seat. She leaned forward, resting her elbows on the backs of the second-row seats.

"I think he's just lonely. And bored."

They all went silent. That was probably the truest statement to fit the bill.

KEEPING TABS

Veronica slumped over her desk in a state of exhaustion. The screen before her showed the tracker on the vehicle she sent with Xander. In the beginning, she was checking the feed every day, her blood pressure heightened by the territories he had to cross. When the medical unit sent a real time report, it took every fiber of her assistant's reasoning to stop her from sending a rescue unit out. From then on, she was only allowed to check on him biweekly. This was one of those days except she felt more at ease.

With the number of companions growing she was sure he could make it to the Litigator alive. After that, it was in the hands of the universe. She was surprised by the Karysilan overriding the vehicle's protocol. It never occurred to her that any of the original creators of those machines would still be around. She was grateful for him showing up when he did.

Alicia came through her office doors in usual hasty fashion. The woman was always in a hurry to get her tasks completed ahead of schedule. She caught a glimpse of Veronica's screen and her lips went thin, slightly crooked.

"What now?" She demanded. "I swear, you keep this up and I will block that feed."

Veronica looked up at her in angered astonishment. She didn't like her tone one bit. As if knowing that, Alicia walked over and leaned down.

"I need you focused. You can't lead if this is going to deter your goals. Or would you rather just hand this facility over to one of those jackasses out there?"

"Don't you dare say that to me!" Veronica slammed a fist on her desk.

"Then get your shit together, boss."

Alicia straightened her glasses and stood.

Veronica regained her composure as well and sat straight in her chair.

"Report."

"When I say jackasses, that means plural enemies."

"Explain."

"One name. Chad Hoskins."

Her chair scraped across the lacquered floor as she stood abruptly. Her eyes glared out the bay window yet she all she could see was red from squinting too hard. With clenched hands, she walked around the desk to stand closer to it. She took a few deep breaths, shaking her hands loose before focusing on the scenery.

"Is he partnered with the New Order?"

Alicia snorted. "Hell no. You think he wants to share glory with anyone? No. He's causing his own havoc out there."

"What the hell is his agenda?"

"As far as taking over facilities, the same. But he wants to essentially segregate regular humans from hybrids and aliens."

"Ugh." Veronica held her stomach. The thought of both factions made her feel sick. "How much time we got?"

"Depends on what your plan is."

"To defend, of course." Veronica turned away from

the window and made eye contact with Alicia. "They will know not to underestimate me."

"Then we're good. Combat units will start being on standby next week."

Both women stood contemplating their roles in the near future. Veronica sneered.

Hoskins, you bastard.

Veronica strolled along the atrium in her personal center with her head down staring at the diamond shaped floor tiles. The light caught them just right, creating prisms. Laughter broke her reverie. She looked up and saw a young girl on the floor, bruises forming on her arms while her son, Caleb, towered over her. He was the one laughing along with Christine standing next to him. She brought up on foot and kicked the girl in the face, sending her flat on the floor.

"Enough!" Veronica stormed towards them and backhanded her daughter. When she fell, clearing the way to her brother, Veronica did him the same. "What is wrong with you?" She turned to the people milling around trying not to stare. "All of you! Is this the kind of home you wanted? We have enemies waiting to take this place and enslave us. If that's the world you want, I will gladly send you all to join them. But as long as you are in my facility, this will NEVER happen again!"

Her son and daughter scooted away, frightened by her demeanor. She could feel herself shaking with rage and knew she must look insane. Bending down, she took a breath and held out her hand.

"Are you okay, sweetie?"

Up close, the girl looked about fourteen. She sat up and stared at Veronica a moment then burst into tears. Some of the people flinched, looking ashamed.

As you should be!

Veronica hugged the girl tight, patting her back. From the corner of her eye she could see her children frown with jealousy. She had coddled them until they were three and sent off for training. Maybe it was a mistake, but she felt the facility was more important.

A staff member assigned as an atrium monitor came to her side and lifted the girl from her arms.

"We'll take care of her from here, Professor."

"Thank you." Veronica stood and faced her children. "Get up!" The crowd dispersed and continued their walks in strained silence. Both wiped their mouths as they did as instructed. "Have you lost your minds?"

"What? Now you give a shit what we do?" Caleb asked.

"If Xander was still around we wouldn't have to find somebody else to mess with." Christine gave her a smirk. That quickly faded.

Veronica grabbed her by the face and in one motion rammed her head into the closest wall ten feet away. No one noticed her move until it was over. Caleb stayed rooted, eyes forward. He didn't dare look back.

"Your brother has more dignity and sense of family than any of you put together. He is out there negotiating for the sake of humanity. What are you doing?"

Veronica let go of her daughter. The girl slid to the floor, tears streaking her face. There was silence. Veronica looked around and saw the people had once again stopped to witness the scene. Guilt consumed her.

"Is that true?" Caleb asked, still not moving. "You sent Xander out there alone?"

"He was the most trustworthy…"

"You sent him out there to die?" He cut her off.

"He's stronger than you'll ever know. I expect him back here."

This time he glanced back at her. His expression that of hate.

"We're nothing but tools for you to use as needed. You could always make more."

He turned and helped his sister up.

"That's not true!" Veronica yelled. "You won't let me love you!"

He let out a loud sigh.

"Because this facility will always be more important than any of us."

Her thoughts thrown back in her face, Veronica staggered back.

"I want to…"

"You think we're monsters," Caleb spat. "So, we prove you right every day. That doesn't mean we don't care what happens to one of our siblings. Xander knew that better than anyone."

Her children walked off, Caleb holding up his sister as they left the commons.

"Professor?" A man with his wife came up to her. "We're being attacked? By who?"

At that moment, her earbud beeped, and Alicia's terse voice came in her ear.

"Boss, I need you to come to your office, right now."

Veronica stared stricken with fear at the man as she realized what she had announced to the entire commons.

"It will be alright. Please, enjoy the rest of your day."

She hurried out of the commons into the lift and went straight to her office.

Once inside, she was met by a very angry assistant. The woman was practically vibrating with hostility. Veronica held up a hand while she went to sit at her desk.

"I know. I have no idea why I did that."

"Oh, I know why you did it. That's still no excuse." Alicia came next to her. "That aside, we have a new problem."

"Oh for god's sake, what now?"

Alicia set her tablet on the desk and the holoscreen above lit up. A feed of data ran down it, sections lighting up in red every few seconds.

"What is this?"

"This happened a few hours ago. Our main frame was sending files to an unknown server. Luckily, the system is smart enough to realize something wasn't right and cut the feed."

"We were hacked?" Veronica swirled around in her chair and stared up at her.

"No, Veronica. This came from our end."

The information sunk in. Veronica's face flushed pink.

"We have a traitor."

"Indeed."

"What did they get?"

"A few weapons inventory, partial schematics and floor blueprints. Personnel designations. Nothing solid, but enough to piece together and do some damage before we can counter."

"Who's in charge of the data? How many?"

"Twenty. Two from each sector. They rotate every quarter, so they have full access."

"Find them. I want to know how they were contacted, by who, and when."

"And after that?"

Murderous intent gleamed in Alicia's eyes. Veronica contemplated if she should greenlight the former assassin. Then she thought about what would happen if the New Order or Hoskins attacked in a week.

"Do whatever makes you happy."

Alicia gave a smile that made Veronica almost feel sorry for the poor bastard who betrayed the facility.

I hope it was worth it! She shouted inward angrily.

New Order vehicles smoldered from damage along the base perimeter. They were broken but repairable. Hoskins wanted every bit of leverage he could get. The fight lasted longer than he wanted, making him feel pissed off at the New Order's audacity. On the floor before him was the leader of the assault. A sniveling man with minimal combat skills as demonstrated when Jesse got him out of his unit. The rest of the New Order scumbags were being held at bay by the more powerful weapons on the base.

Hoskins knocked the side of the man's head with bare knuckles and squinted.

"Now, I'm a bit confused about this whole New Order thing. What the hell are you all thinking? This whole," Hoskins pointed up and twirled his finger, "balls in approach ain't working for you."

"We tried the nice approach. We're done with that. People need to comply with our demands and start acting like goddamn human beings! Not animals!"

"Oh, I agree with you on that."

"Then why are you getting in our way?"

Hoskins leaned forward until he hovered over the man. They made eye contact.

"You want everyone to sing kumbaya together and form some utopia. News flash. There aren't just humans on this rock anymore. And no, we don't get along as well as you think."

"And what? You think segregation is the answer? They did that in the nineteenth and twentieth centuries. Look how that ended."

Hoskins punched him in the face. The man's head snapped back, and his body began to slump. Two soldiers grabbed him under the arms and held him up. Blood trickled from his nose.

He straightened his stance.

"I'm not talking about that bullshit! We can do better than that."

One of Hoskins' soldiers came into the command center with a tablet in hand. He set it on the communications console and the giant vidscreen above changed images.

"Got this from the combat unit this guy was in. We were able to link to the main system and get some info before its defense protocol locked us out."

The man's eyes went wide then he sucked air between his teeth. Hoskins grinned.

"Didn't want us to know about stuff? Too bad." He turned to the soldier. "Whatcha' got?"

"Locations, sir. Along with some pretty specific intel on each one."

"Which ones?"

"Facility three, Mecca," the soldier paused and looked over at him. "Metropolis."

Hoskins sat back and rubbed his lower lip. Metropolis. A massive hold run by that former Terror his father didn't tame or dispose of. The weapons and comm system in that thing alone could connect the entire planet. He would have a worldwide operation in mere months. From the look on the prisoner's face, they were thinking the same thing.

"See? This is why you guys are fucking up. Instead of hitting all these small potatoes, you should have beefed up all your forces and hit this one hard."

"And that's where you're wrong." The man spat blood on the floor. "Information is key. We got spies in Mecca and Facility three is easy to infiltrate. Metropolis takes more time."

"You know, I was gonna' shoot ya.'"

"Then do it," the man demanded.

"Nah!" Hoskins got up and stood under the giant

vidscreen. "I'm going to fix up those machines and take all y'all to Metropolis with me."

"You're going to get us all killed!"

Hoskins smirked.

"Nope. Just you New Order people. I'll already be inside taking over when they're through with you." His stare darkened. "And I'll get rid of that shitty Terror defector."

He remembered the last time he saw Terence was in the Terror recruitment compound. His father had let him come see the candidates. A group of soldiers were trying to wrestle Terence down into a storage room around the corner where he stood. Their eyes met and Terence reached out, pleading for him to help. They finally got him on the ground, forcing him to shift with multiple punches and kicks. One of the soldiers was already getting a few strokes in when a commanding officer came to the doorway screaming and yelling for them to get back to their stations.

The commanding officer had another group of soldiers get Terence off the floor. Chad realized his father was no longer by his side. Next to the commanding officer, he found his father grabbing one of the soldiers by the front of his uniform.

"You think I'm running some kind of whorehouse?"

"No sir!"

"No one touches these recruits, you understand?"

"Yes sir!"

"I brought that thing here to be a killing machine for America. Soldiers don't lower themselves to fucking nonhumans. They might as well go screwing goats and shit!"

"I understand, sir. My apologies, sir. I will make sure the men know."

His father released the officer and came back to

stand by his side. The presenter was still talking about the timeline for deploying the Terrors.

"You alright, boss?" Jesse was standing next to him.

Hoskins cleared his throat and nodded.

"Yeah. Just thinking of the past for a minute."

Yep. The moment that incident happened; he knew that Terror was going to be a liability. It just took almost two decades before Terence implemented his mutiny. A lot of American soldiers died in that fight for the Terrors' so-called freedom.

"Let's get this show on the road. Metropolis needs some cleansing."

SERENDIPITY

Barren land stretched for miles.

Kevin grimaced. Two months of traveling the vast sand and wastelands of the Gobi Desert had him still feeling ashamed and guilty for his actions at Metropolis. The look on his older children's faces was enough to let him know he needed to leave. He didn't dare go near Terence as she held their unconscious ten-year-old son close to her body.

"What the fuck is wrong with me?" He adjusted the messenger bag with dual straps on his shoulders and kicked at the hard-caked ground. "I'll make it right. I promise you."

His trench coat was covered in dust, the faux leather already worn. It lay open exposing the black battlesuit underneath. A thick black scarf was wrapped around his head and face to combat the harsh wind blowing debris. So far, there was no shelter in sight. From what he could gather from the lay of the land, one should appear in the next twenty miles.

Fuck, that's a long walk!

The view goggles were also covered in dust. He used a gloved finger to wipe the lenses. Ten miles out the weather was different yet again. He stared up at the sky. Swirls of colors moved in every direction. Where it was darker, with angry red clouds, he could make out rainfall. Thanking his luck for moving the opposite way, he trekked on.

After what seemed like eternity, he finally arrived at the halfway point and into clear skies. The air was cleaner too. Kevin unwrapped the scarf and took off the messenger bag. He shoved the scarf in then took off his coat, rolling it into a tight tube before pushing it into the bag as well. Putting the bag back on, he raised the goggles off his face and set them atop his head. The air felt good on his eyes. He remembered seeing the temperature in the goggle's display, a mild mid-sixty degrees Fahrenheit.

Perfect.

He continued his long walk through the territory heading for the shelter that should be coming up soon. He was tired.

Hours went by slowly, yet he persevered. There was no other choice. He caught sight of what looked like a structure off in the distance and let out a sigh of relief. Until he smelled something familiar.

Iron.

Blood curdling screams from up ahead carried on the wind towards him, stopping Kevin in his tracks. He stood still, scanning the wide-open area around him to make sure nothing was close. The audible assault was followed by crunching, snapping sounds. By his calculation, it was a good two miles away. The only reason he could hear it was due to him purposely heightening his senses. In the wastelands, surprises were not something to be fond of.

Adjusting his vision, he saw a ridge blocking off a section of the open range. The sounds were coming from there. Directly in his travel path. He proceeded with caution, his steps lighter than before. A small breeze swept up some of the dry spots on the ground creating small whirlwinds.

As he rounded the edge of the ridge, he came upon a blood bath long over. He counted at least five bodies. Intact. Body parts were strewn across the surface. Large splotches of blood peppered the area. He had to step over a few to go further in. Crunching, smacking. The sound of something wet and sticky.

Sitting on a broken slab of concrete that was once part of a building was a man with long chestnut curls, legs wide apart. In his hands was as human forearm nearly stripped of tissue to the bone. Blood was smeared up to the man's elbows.

Kevin, not one to fear much, got a little closer for a good look at him. He gasped, stepping back a few feet. His eyes widened in disbelief, glancing around at the carnage, then back at the man. He recognized him from the government database he hacked before the war.

"What," he asked slowly, "are you doing?"

Yellow eyes looked up at him through wet wavy bangs. George, the former Head of Homeland Security for the United States, dropped the severed forearm. He swiped a bloody finger through his lips, sucking some of the residue off as it exited the other side of his mouth.

"Having a bit of lunch," he replied calmly. Kevin glared at him. "Mmm, that's right. You skipped this stage of your evolution."

Kevin had heard that Senigrankes began as carnivores, feasting on other species throughout the galaxy until they evolved into Litigators. He was a halfbreed and therefore an anomaly. In all his life, he had never actually seen a full blooded one eat someone.

"Why?" Kevin raised his arms and gestured towards the torn limbs scattered about.

George wiped his mouth with the sleeve of his weather worn shirt and stood to his full height of six feet seven inches. His eyes flickered and turned a dark grey.

He wore leather leggings shiny from the bloody wetness and black boots that came just below his knees. The long black robe lay on the slab next to him.

"Believe me, you would not want to deal with these heathens. Plus," he grinned, "they pissed me off. Tried to rob and kill me."

Kevin tried to picture the group of renegades coming across a lone unarmed man walking the wastelands and deciding this was the guy to target. It made no sense. They were asking to be slaughtered. Then he thought about himself in the same situation. He would have brought them all down in one hit.

George walked towards Kevin and stopped mere inches from him. Kevin was a little over six foot three. George towered over him. Then he remembered, George used to play college basketball.

"Care to join me?" George asked.

"What?" Kevin leaned away. "I am not a maneater. Just, no!"

George cocked his head to one side and smiled.

"That's not what I meant, genius."

"Oh." Kevin felt his face flush. "Right."

"There is plenty left if you want to try a hand at it."

Kevin gagged.

"Come. I think we're both looking for the same being."

"You're going to look for the Litigator? Aren't the two of you on the same page being both Senigrankes?"

"He's evolved, I'm not. And, yes, I want to talk to him about this planet."

"Yeah, but will he see reason when we get there to try and persuade him?"

"We can always eat him." George flashed a bloody teeth smile.

Kevin stared at him in disbelief then defeat.

That's right. Senigrankes also eat their own kind.

"Okay. First things first." Kevin pointed to the building ahead. "I need to rest."

George smirked but nodded.

"Agreed. You look like shit." He stared at him intently. "And not just because you've been walking the Earth for months on end."

"I'm not talking about it. I'm tired." His voice was almost a whimper.

The two headed towards the building and to their surprise, its integrity was intact. They went inside and found themselves in what used to be a weapons storage. Most of the walls were bare but a few assault rifles still sat on the racks. Further in was a small room with bunk beds and a shelf unit of rations that had been ransacked. A few packets lay scattered.

"It's not real food, but it will do for now," Kevin said, palming one of the packets.

George looked at it dubiously.

"Whatever makes you happy."

Kevin shook the packet until it started to heat up and he laid on the nearest bottom bunk. His eyes nearly closed before he remembered the packet, now piping hot in his hand. He sat up, tore it open and poured the contents in his mouth.

"What is that supposed to be anyway?" George glanced at the wording on the pouch. "Never did like those damn things."

"I think it says turkey dinner or something," Kevin mumbled. His eyes refused to stay open. "Don't you fucking try to eat me either."

As he fell asleep, he saw George's eyes turn yellow with a grin spread across his face.

⌒

Wisps of energy swirled around him like stardust. The universe spread before him like a kaleidoscope of wonder. There was no sense of his physical body yet he had a thought that he was floating. The stars became streaks of light and he appeared to travel great distances until it stopped in a solar system he had never seen before. A large planet pulsing the slightest pale green glow with a wide band that went through the entire half. But the other side was a perpetual dark, forever blocked from the muted sun sitting so far away. He reached out to embrace the strange new world.

No! You cannot!

The voice seared into his mind, stopping his motion instantly. The pain spread and he started to scream.

"Stop!"

Kevin rose from the bed holding both sides of his face as blood dripped from his eyes and nostrils. His breathing was hard and heavy, making his chest hurt.

"Stop!"

George grabbed hold of his elbows and squeezed.

"Snap out of it! Kevin!"

He let his eyes focus and the room came into full view. Tears tinted with blood fell onto his lap. He wrenched himself away from George and swung his legs off the bed.

"What was that?" George asked.

"A dream, I guess."

"No," George replied. "Not that." Kevin looked up at him. "The power surge that flooded the place while you thrashed around in your sleep."

"Huh?"

"Get up. We have to leave. I smell people coming. About a day or two away."

Kevin's eyes went wide.

"You can smell humans that far away?"

"Did you forget? We can open pathways through the galaxy when we get a whiff of prey. A few days away is nothing compared to an entire solar system."

Kevin narrowed his eyes at him.

"I won't let you."

George let out a guffaw. When he was done, he gave Kevin a sly look.

"Try and stop me." George laughed again. "Let's go. I'll restrain myself for your benefit." He stopped at the entrance. "And wipe your face. All that blood is getting to me."

"Yeah, sure."

Kevin found a packet of wipes laying around and broke the seal. He used a couple to thoroughly wipe his face them stuck the rest of the pack in his satchel. On the way out, he grabbed a few more MREs. George shook his head and snorted.

"Unlike you, I need real food."

"That isn't even real food," George countered.

True. I'll give him that.

The two made their way towards the Litigator's location. His energy pulsating out like a signal was their guide. The Litigator was making no attempts to hide. Kevin squinted as they passed the territory's threshold and entered another with sunlight. But his eyesight was different. Strange halos surrounded everything in his peripheral. He blinked a few times to no avail. George tilted his head in an angle away from him.

"Too bright?"

Kevin pinched the bridge of his nose and squeezed his eyes shut for a moment. When he opened them, the halo was still there.

"Sure."

"It's barely casting enough light to create shadows."

George's tone was terse.

He took hold of Kevin's bicep and yanked him.

"What's going on?"

Kevin stared at him, his eyes trying to see…what? George let go and stepped away from him. A strange dark aura, razor thin, shimmered in and out of focus around George. Kevin resumed walking. George followed a few feet away.

"You've traveled this galaxy. Have you ever seen a planet split in half by its rings?" He heard Georges footsteps halt. He also stopped and turned to him.

"Explain." George's eyes had a hint of green glow. "What did it look like?"

"One side was, well, it was the same color your eyes are right now. The other side was almost hidden it was so dark. The sun's rays didn't quite reach it."

"That," George hissed, "is Granada. Our homeworld." "Wha…?"

"You tried to go there. That's what that surge was." George was on him in flash. "Don't ever do that again." His voice was soft and teeming with venom. Their eyes locked. George's face turned to shock. "What do you see?"

Kevin jerked from his grip.

"Why? Why can't I go there?" He yelled.

"Cuz, you'll die! They'll rip you apart to see what makes you different." George stepped closer. "Make no mistake, you are indeed different."

To Kevin's surprise, George reached out and ran a hand down the side of his face. The spell was broken as they both heard the humming of an engine coming from up ahead. George's eyes changed to yellow.

"No! You said you would not eat anyone."

"I said I would try to restrain myself."

"George!"

"Fine. I'll only take a limb."

Kevin frowned.

"A chunk. How about that?" George aked snarkily.

A modified tank came roaring over the horizon with people leaning out of it brandishing weapons. These were not sophisticated hoodlums with advanced combat gear. Nope. They were straight out of a twentieth century post-apocalyptic film. A random group of regular humans who happened to survive after refusing to evacuate. Kevin changed his mind.

"A few bites may or may not kill anyone."

"Save you some?" George quipped.

"No, thank you!"

"Not going to use your power?"

"That would be a waste. I'm just going to kick their asses to kingdom come."

As the hoodlums got closer, Kevin took a few deep breaths.

No need to go overboard.

Kevin winced as George leaned down and punched through the man's chest, ripping out his heart. The other fighters had already sped off with their wounded, leaving the dying man to such a cruel fate. He would have been dead in a few minutes anyway and Kevin felt he had suffered enough. George apparently thought so too. He stood with the organ beating twice more before going still then bit into it. Blood splattered outward, some of it spraying onto Kevin.

"Fuck, George! Don't just eat it right in front of me!"

George wasn't listening. His expression oozed euphoria with every bite. Kevin forced himself not to gag. He knew what was coming next. There would be no argument from him. George wasn't going to let the fresh carnage go to waste. Kevin saw George's aura change color and get a little thicker.

Hours of walking side by side, their gaits matching as they traveled, led them to a small stream. A ribbon of murky water less than three feet deep giving off a slight rancid odor. Regardless, George used it to wash the baked-on blood from his hand and face. Kevin reluctantly did the same. The sun had not moved. Its rays were steady and over time made the air hot. Even the water, where its direct line of sight landed, felt heated.

"From the looks of it, I don't think we can drink this." Kevin wrinkled his nose at the smell. "I do have conversion tabs."

"This is from rain. You definitely don't want to drink it." George finished washing his face and stood. He scanned the area, following the stream. "It's getting better."

Kevin got up from knees.

"Which will be all for nothing if the Litigator has his way."

"We're close. Another week or so and we'll be face to face with the man himself."

"I wanna' wring his neck."

"That's not how to negotiate." George turned back to the hill they had climbed over to get to the stream. "Chop, chop."

Kevin followed him down back to the vast open terrain. Not one blade of grass.

A day later they came across a bunker hidden in a sand hill. George snorted as they reached the entrance.

"We have so many of these all over the planet for situations like this."

Kevin gave him a dirty stare.

"And what situation would that be?"

"Oh, you know, stranded in the desert with no way to get across the water."

"Is that right?"

George brushed packed sand off the side of the entrance frame to reveal a touch pad. He entered a code and the door unsealed, sliding open to the left. The two were met with darkness.

"Looks like the motion sensors are malfunctioning." He walked further in while Kevin waited outside. Light emitted from the opening and George called out to him. "Come on in. You have to see the goods."

Kevin frowned as he proceeded inside. A stairwell went down about one hundred feet and stopped at an open space in the bunker. Five skimmer vehicles sat along the walls. A closer inspection found only three were capable of travel.

"Looks like the previous guests didn't want to be followed. This bunker held ten of these. With two of the remaining sabotaged, it must have been a dire issue." George circled the space and noticed the bare sections of wall where weapons would have been stored. "And a pretty good fight too."

"Well, let's get going. How much energy fuel do these things have?"

George straddled one and hit the start sequence button. He went through the skimmer's menu and came to the gauge.

"Barely enough to get us on the other side. The unit is damaged. It's been leaking energy for a while." He went over to the one next to it and checked that one. "Same here."

"If they were being chased by those crazy fuckers we ran into back there, I can understand why they did it."

George hit the hangar release and the top of the bunker split in two as each side lifted open to the let in the night sky. Sand shifted across the sides, trickling in. He got on his skimmer followed by Kevin mounting his own and they started to hover. The skimmers rose until they cleared the top of the doors. George waited for them to seal back shut then gave Kevin a nod. Together they engaged the thrusters and took off towards the edge of the continent.

They arrived at the shore of an area once known as Kimchaek and could see the broken island of Japan off in the horizon. Kevin watched the water churn, its beauty lessened by the low levels and contamination. They stopped for a moment taking in the scenery.

"This is so fucked up," Kevin said.

"I agree. Your waters were indeed beautiful." George let out a heavy sigh. "Let's get there quick before our energy cells run out and we end up dropping midway. I know how to swim. I just don't want to do that right now."

Kevin let out a muffled laugh.

"Me either."

They resumed their race across the Sea of Japan, keeping an eye on the fuel cells. When they reached one percent, both George and Kevin looked up at the emerging shoreline still a half mile away. The skimmers started to sputter and jerk, descending towards the water due to their riders' weight.

"Aw, damn!"

The skimmers hit the water and bounced across the stop as their gauges showed zero fuel. A quarter mile to go. Kevin's eyes glowed and a swell formed behind them. George gripped the handles of his skimmer harder in anticipation of Kevin's handy work. The swell rammed into the backs of the skimmers, pushing the dead machines to the rest of the way. They hit land hard, the skimmers breaking apart as they careened against rocks embedded in the sand. Both men were tossed in the air and dumped face first mere feet from a cliff.

Kevin moved his hands to his sides and pushed

himself up, spitting out sand and pieces of twigs. George shook his head to get most of the debris out of his hair before getting to his feet.

"Well, that was entertaining," George said. He turned yellow eyes towards Kevin. "How about we not do that again?"

"It got us to shore, didn't it?" Kevin stood, brushing sand off his clothes. "Did you have a better idea?" He saw the look on George's face. "Besides swimming for it?"

"Nope." George pointed to Kevin's messenger bag. "You better check that. Make sure nothing is damaged."

Kevin pulled the bag off and let the water drip from it. The material was waterproof but he wasn't sure it could withstand submersion. He opened and checked the contents. Everything was surprising still dry.

"All good."

"Great." George propped himself against the cliff wall. "Now I need a rest."

Kevin tapped his wristband and set an alarm for six hours. He figured by that time it would be late in the morning and better sunlight. Within minutes, he too was laid up next to George sound asleep.

The high-pitched tinging of Kevin's wristband going off with the timer made George bolt upright to scan the area. He regained his composure and looked over at the thing making noise. He smacked Kevin in the arm.

"Turn that thing off."

Kevin stirred from sleep, slow to rise then heard the annoying racket as well. He jolted from the sound then tapped the wristband in frustration as he missed the cancel icon twice before getting it. The alarm off, he got to his feet along with George. They took stock of the cliff.

"Ready to climb up and see what kind of territory we got to explore?" Kevin asked.

"Sure. Why not." George gestured with one hand. "After you."

Kevin obliged and headed up. At the top, he pulled himself over the ledge. He stood there staring at the terrain. George came up beside him and grimaced as he too glanced around.

Nothing. As far as the eye could see.

"At least the sky is clear, and the temperature is mild." Kevin tried to sound cheerful. George glared at him. "Fine. Onward."

They started their journey across Japan in the direction of the Litigator.

The territory ended with a sharp change in weather. Wind churned at nearly thirty miles an hour and dusty chunks of debris fly everywhere. Kevin was brought to one knee as he tried to shield his face. For a few seconds, it let up and he was able to get his goggles out of his bag. The two men had noticed the darkened sky ahead of them and had prepared by donning their heavier gear. Their heads and mouths were wrapped up good and their coats fully sealed shut. This was worse than they had anticipated. Kevin adjusted the goggles until they sat right on his face and zoomed in.

Dark funnels zig zagged across the territory, lightning sparking out from their tops. The ground had been gouged all over from being torn up by the funnels' path. George was standing silent assessing the situation. Kevin made a waving motion with two fingers towards where they came from. They could back track and find another way around the territory. It would lengthen their travel by another week.

Through the already dusty goggles he could see George's eyes narrow at him. Kevin dropped his shoulders in submission and stood arms raised. His entire body glowed a pale green and he focused on the funnels. Three of them began to unravel, dissipating into dust. One of the farthest funnels suddenly changed trajectory, growing bigger, and headed straight for Kevin. It bent until he could see its core, black and unyielding.

That made Kevin angry. He pushed his will against it while he conjured enough clouds to create rain. There was resistance. Some of the clouds refused to combine.

The Litigator.

Kevin let out a roar of frustration that got muffled through the wrapping.

Let me through! He demanded.

Mustering more energy, Kevin's fingers curled, and a shot of light emitted from his body, hitting the funnels head on. They broke apart followed by the rain he had requested of the clouds. Each drop sizzled on the ground. The Litigator's present.

"Fuck!" Kevin yelled through his covered mouth.

They were in the open with no shelter in sight. Their clothing began to smoke. George grabbed him by the back of his coat collar and tossed him over the threshold of the previous territory. He took one look at the sky then ran back to where Kevin landed with a thud, rolling on his side to a stop.

George unraveled his head wrap and knelt by him.

"Looks like you pissed him off. Or, he's toying with you."

Kevin slammed his fists on the ground as he lay staring at the sky. He finally unwrapped his face and took in a deep breath.

"That son of a bitch!"

His breathless voice conveyed his rage.

"Come on. I guess he's not ready for us. We have to go around."

"I don't want to do what HE wants!" Kevin yelled.

"Well, we have no choice, do we?"

Kevin sat up and let George pull him up by the hand. Back in the sunlight, they began to undo their gear and revert to lesser outerwear. Wrappings and coats stowed, they headed to the right, circumventing the hostile territory.

∽

Atop a hillside stripped of life in a territory that was once called Nagoya, Roland sat observing the new territories below. There were four of them about fifty miles apart in each direction and different in every way. He found it fascinating the course each community took to regain some semblance of living. Since livestock was no longer an option, most humans adopted a vegan diet. Nearly every community had set up greenhouses and traded seeds with other territories. Then there were the others who deemed human flesh was just as good. Roland had to agree, having eaten a few humans over the past few decades. Despite that, he thought of them as subhuman. The lowest form of humans who didn't deserve to live.

He turned his attention to the West. His vision zoomed in on George and Kevin trekking across the desolate earth. George seemingly still put out from the tornados he had unleashed, and Kevin very much enraged by it, his face contorted in a permanent frown. Roland snickered at the young hybrids state. The detour would nearly double their amount of time to reach him.

"I won't make this easy." He glanced back at the four hubs full of people below. "These humans are not persuading me one bit."

At sunset, one of the modified vehicles came roaring out of the makeshift town farther out and headed towards the next one. Roland's eyes narrowed, glowing pale green. The last time the ventured out, another town was left devastated, some of their people taken while others were butchered. He watched as the horde dragged a woman they had kidnapped to a podium and chopped her up alive. They made stew from her that night.

That part is what appalled Roland. The unnecessary cruelty they went through to eat their own kind. It was aesthetically unappealing. Senigrankes had neurotoxin they injected with the first bite so that by the time they were deep in consumption, their prey was no longer in crisis. Too much adrenaline and tense muscles made the meat taste bad. Humans had no sense of etiquette.

He thought about what he should do to deter them. He had seen enough from them. A storm would sweep them up and dumped them on the ground. But he wanted them to feel something more than a few broken bones. To know how their prey felt. To suffer. For the first time since he set up the hillside as his temporary home, he decided to go down into the territory.

The field of energy formed a bubble around him as he floated across the plains. When he reached the edge of the first town, he landed gently on the ground and dissolved the energy. He continued on foot to the main gates. Along the perimeter he could hear the metal clanging of alarms sounding. The lookout was atop the post wearing enhanced goggles watching the vehicle approach. Roland went to the center of the main gates and stood, waiting. No one could see him in the closing darkness of night.

He knew from previous encounters the town had learned from other incidents and would open the gates for no one. They had done that once and paid the price.

The enemy vehicle was still a good half a kilometer away when it fired a missile from its front cannon.

"Incoming!" He heard the lookout shout down at the gathering forces on the other side of the gate. "It's gonna' blow a hole right through! Be ready!"

Not on my watch.

Roland formed a circle of air than picked up speed as it spun. He turned it sideways as the missile came in range and let it go. The missile sliced apart clean down the center and the two pieces flew in opposite directions before detonating. There were cries of anticipation for the impending doom, then confused rumblings. The smoke cleared and he saw the occupants of the vehicle none too happy about his interference. Above him, the lookout finally saw what was going on and climbed down.

"Take cover!"

"Good idea," Roland said more to himself.

Three of the enemy jumped out of the vehicle while it was still moving, weapons drawn. The first charged towards him with the other two not far behind.

"This ain't your business, trekker. This ain't your town." The man yelled it as he ran making his voice sound gruffer than it probably was. "Gonna teach you the business."

He stopped short a few yards from Roland and raised a handmade weapon. Pristine alloy formed in a razor-sharp arc at the top section and the other end a sharp spear. No matter which side he used, it was deadly. Roland waited for the vehicle to stop so the rest of them could get out. The first assailant was within a few feet of him. He smiled, angering the man further.

The man let out a battle cry, leaping into the air with the arc pointed towards Roland. The rest of the enemy fighters made a beeline for the main gate, circumventing him. Or so they thought.

Roland's eyes glowed once more.

He snapped a finger. The man's weapon broke in half and he appeared to bounce off an invisible barrier. He conjured up multiple wisps of air, weaving them into a net around him.

"Fucking alien!" The man spat blood onto the ground where he landed. "Kill that mother…"

The net of wind spread out like a pulse, touching everything in its wake. Deep cuts covered the main gate, causing fractures, yet it held. The wind dissipated, leaving a lull of silence. Roland stepped towards his assailant and loomed over him. They made eye contact. He knew what the man was thinking.

Don't move.

Roland saw he understood the pain and horror he was about to experience. Tiny red lines formed a checkered pattern across the man's body. Right as he got a scream out, his arm fell apart in chunks. More screams followed from the other enemy fighters. Roland watched with disinterest as one of the men, tears and snot covering his face begged for mercy before his torso slid apart onto the ground. He picked up a chunk, brushed it off and took a bite.

"Not bad. Could use a little more despair."

He finished off the chunk and walked back towards his hillside. As expected, the second vehicle came up to the scene, assessed the situation, and began to scoop up the remains of their comrades. The goal of acquiring fresh meat was met in their eyes. Beggars can't be choosy. Disgusted by the display, Roland floated up to the sky. He saw the town still hunkered down on the other side of the main gate. The look out and a few others stared at him then nodded.

That's the last time.

CHAPTER FOUR

GROUP EFFORT

A dust cloud far off in the distance got George and Kevin's attention. They were in the middle of nowhere still steaming from having to divert back the way they came, then curve around the territory of tornadoes. George knew of a presence closing in on them. Now it was multiplied. His wide range sense of smell counted four bodies ripe for eating. One scent he knew almost instantly. He breathed it in a little more to confirm. Karysilan.

Tasty.

Kevin stopped a few feet behind him. When he turned to see why, he was met with a look of utter disdain. The young hybrid's eyes glowed that pale green Litigators had and narrowed at him.

"What is wrong with you now?"

"You are not eating anybody," Kevin's voice seethed.

George rolled his eyes upwards before staring back at him.

"They could be an enemy. Would you still say that?"

"Yes." Kevin's face contorted in anger.

"Fine." George let out a heavy sigh. "Suit yourself." He glanced off to the side of Kevin and saw the dust cloud getting closer. "I say they're about an hour away. Want to keep walking or wait for them?"

Kevin glared up at the sky. He smelled rain. The bad kind. Even if they kept walking, there was no shelter in sight for miles. They had protective gear but no idea how long it would last in a continuous rain shower.

"I guess we don't have a choice."

George watched Kevin's expression turn to submission as he dropped his gear on the ground and pulled out the rain cover. He didn't like that look. Then again, Kevin was too young. A mere infant by his and other races' standards. Like a child pouting when they don't get what they want. The rain would start in twenty minutes which meant they would have to endure it for another forty until their pursuers arrived.

"Well, let's get comfy."

George pulled out a small packet from his coat and opened it. The rain cover sailed out. He put it over his coat and flipped the hood that extended four inches from his face.

"Let me guess," Kevin said. "Extra-large."

"Triple XL, to be accurate." George smirked. "I'm a big guy." This time Kevin rolled his eyes, giving him a side stare. "Maybe our new friends will have some provisions you can pilfer."

"Or maybe," Kevin replied vehemently, "they don't want to stop in the rain and will pass us by. I know that's what I would do."

George sat and observed Kevin even as the needle like rain came pouring down, singeing the rain cover. Not acid rain, but just as smelly and dangerous. Something about Kevin gave him pause. He had a theory about his origin. If he was right, the situation would be made all the more hellish.

Kevin was either asleep or meditating. He sat legs crossed, his hands laid flat atop each other while his head was bowed to let the rain run off. His eyes closed, he appeared so serene, his breathing slow and steady.

Childlike.

Shaking his head to clear his thoughts, George looked away and did the same. He needed to calm himself. Hunger pains were coming, and he decided to comply with Kevin's wishes. Unless they proved hostile. Then all bets were off.

The white vehicle came into view and George let out a whistle. It was larger than he expected. He recognized its model. I'll be damned. They were made for combat envoys and only a few compounds had them. Kevin opened his eyes and turned to the approaching behemoth. It stopped fifty yards from them, the wheels tossing black mud. They both stood. A standoff ensued. No one came out of the vehicle and they didn't move either.

After what felt like eternity, the hatch doors of the vehicle finally opened. Two people came out to stand by its sides. George made a sharp intake of breath. The Karysilan he smelled was one he knew well. He stepped forward.

"Grannalt."

Grannalt seemed surprised and backed away.

"How do you know me?" His voice quivered.

"Because I worked for the President of the United States and knew about all the terrible projects we conducted on your race. Especially you." Grannalt's hands balled into fist. He scanned the other man and cocked his head. "Bioengineered combat class. I'd know that DNA anywhere. Where are you from?"

"Mecca."

"Ah, Australia. That means you're one of Headland's children."

"Correct. I am Xander Headland."

"Are you done?"

Kevin was staring at him in astonished anger.

"Whether you know them is irrelevant. We going down fighting or what?"

"Assessing probability of success." The vehicle AI interrupted. "Combatants are high level. Chance of surviving combat against them less than two percent. Advise retreat."

"Shut up!" Grannalt snapped. "No one is fighting anybody!" He turned to George and Kevin. "Do you want to get out of this shitty rain or not?"

Kevin's head tilted back as if he had been hit. George stifled a laugh. He grabbed Kevin by the arm.

"Let's go. No need to reject a perfect gift."

George had to duck his head under the doorway to climb in. Kevin followed and they both settled in the middle section. George looked back and saw the two young ones in the back. They smelled delicious. The hatch doors closed, sealing everyone in and the vehicle took off.

"Running signature analysis." The vehicle AI said.

"Uh oh," George laughed.

"Signature one. Kevin Lang. Assistant to Professor Morandi, Italy Facility. Combat class talent user. Designation Litigator."

"What?" Xander and Grannalt exclaimed.

"Clarification. This is not the Litigator we are seeking."

Kevin went slackjawed. George burst out laughing. When he recovered, he placed a hand over his face.

"So, you're all going to try and persuade that bastard as well. Talk about serendipity."

"Signature two. George Huntsman. Head of Homeland Security, the United States of America, under President Rebecca Lynmore. High level talent user. Designation Senigranke."

This time everyone seemed to crawl away from him, fear in their eyes.

"No need to worry. I was told not to eat anyone this time." He gave Kevin a crooked smile. Kevin frowned. "So hungry," George sighed. He turned to the two in the back. "And what are your names?"

"Those are my children!"

"Yes, yes. Glad you found some of them. Why are you being defensive when I already said I wasn't eating any of you?" His eyes turned yellow as he turned his attention on the two. "I'll ask again."

"My name is Seth." The young man pointed to the girl clinging to him in fright. "This is my sister, Erin. Our mother is overly protective. We're not really afraid of you."

To confirm that fact, Erin stuck her tongue out at him. George's eyes returned to normal.

"Hmph. You should be."

Kevin finally relaxed in the seat and exhaled slowly. He addressed Xander.

"Since we have the same goal, is it fair to say we can hitch a ride for the duration?"

"That would be ideal," Xander replied. "We do have a slight snag in our mission."

"The New Order."

"You know about them?" Xander turned towards him. "Their goal is to kill him."

"They would need a god killer," Seth said.

"Or another Senigranke," George added. They all stared at him. "But, even that's a long shot. He's evolved. Like Seth says, he's on a god level."

"So, they're delusional," Erin stated.

"Pretty much." Grannalt settled in the front seat.

The tension subsided, they waited for the display screen to update the rendezvous time to the Litigator. A tube packet tapped against George's shoulder. He turned his head to see Erin frowning as she continued tapping.

"You eat regular food too, right? Eat this so you don't starve."

He took the tube and read the label on the side. High concentrated Polenta. Kevin looked over and made a retching gesture.

"What? You don't like this? I lived for this stuff. Made my base near the Mexican border." He broke open the top and pushing the contents up bit off the entire section. "Mmm. This is better than I thought."

"See?" Erin smiled. Then her expression grew dark. "Now you don't have to eat people."

For the next ten days, the newly formed group of six got to know each other better by talking and eating together. Erin was constantly forcing George to eat something as a deterrent. He indulged her. Seth and Xander barely talked to anyone so they bonded that way. During a pit stop in a sunny part of the territory, Grannalt walked with Kevin.

"You have the same powers as the Litigator?"

"Not quite." Kevin raised his hands and looked at them. "I couldn't force him back. He's way stronger than I am. He was only toying with me in that tornado storm I mentioned earlier."

"We saw that on the typography screen. It was massive. And a miracle you got out of there in one piece."

"If I push it," Kevin paused afterwards. "I have no idea what my limits are. Never tried to find out."

"And you shouldn't. For all you know, the two of you clashing could cause a catastrophe."

Kevin halted mid step. That had never occurred to him.

"Then what do we do if he doesn't listen? We can't let him murder a bunch of New Order people either."

"You can stop those idiots. No need for him to get involved."

"Hmm."

"I smell an enemy coming," George said, coming out of the vehicle.

"I didn't see anything on the radar." Xander checked the screen. His expression turned to shock. "It's moving really fast."

Within seconds, they all heard the loud sizzle of thrusters. A large hovercraft came into view and slowed to a crawl before settling near them.

"That's a third-generation combat class transport," George announced. He noticed the crude modifications on the hull and weapons. "They messed it all up."

"They obviously don't have any idea how to use the damn thing," Grannalt added.

"Yeah, but it can hold up to thirty soldiers."

The side hatch opened, and twelve men and women clambered out with weapons. They wore the usual fare of combat suits adorned with handmade accessories. One of them had a metal piece that sat on his head like a crown. In his hand was a blade that could cut through biotech fabric. Seth and Erin backed away.

Grannalt grabbed Kevin by the arm.

"Those guys must be from the same faction as those fuckers who tried to carve up my kids. Be careful."

"Then why are they this far out on another continent? Is it some kind of clan thing? How far has this shit spread?" Kevin stepped up to stand by George. "This is ridiculous."

"What we got, what we got," the man said as he swung the blade back and forth at his side. "Nice vehicle. Sleek and all that." He tilted his head back at an angle, his gaze never leaving the group. "Think we need it, y'all?"

"Absolutely, Kingman," they answered.

One of the enemy stepped forward.

"We could use a new ride."

"I take it back," Erin whispered.

"What?" Kevin asked, confused.

"You should eat them. All of them."

George stared at her for a moment, not sure if she was serious, then saw the terror in her eyes. He had heard Grannalt tell the story of what they could see on the display as the vehicle raced towards them. The one thing that angered him the most was hearing about the skull necklace. And when he turned back to the horde of enemy fighters, he saw one of them had one around his neck.

"As you wish."

Kevin's expression changed from worry to resignation. The enemy charged at them.

"Let's take care of this," he told the rest of the group.

He gave George a nod. Eyes glowing pale green, Kevin conjured up a miniature whirlwind. Some of the fighters skidded to a halt and reared back. Kevin released the whirlwind, knocking half the enemy back against the hovercraft. The weapons system came online, and the cannon eye moved until it targeted the group. Before it could fire, Grannalt was on top of it and rammed one of his cylinders through the bubble. He leapt off as it exploded. Four more enemy fighters came running out, their clothes scorched.

Grannalt fought with them while four other enemy fighters went after Xander, Seth, and Erin. George zeroed in on a fighter. Bigger than the rest, he was on par in size with him. Meaty. With a flash step, George was on the man. He held him down by the throat, the man punching him in the face continuously in an effort to make him let go. George smiled, eyes glowing yellow.

"So hungry," he breathed.

He opened wide and took a giant chunk out of the man's shoulder. The sound of bone crunching between his teeth seemed to echo around him. The taste of fresh prey sent him in a state of euphoria. He chewed a few times before swallowing then took a second bite right under the armpit. The man still struggled but his strength was fading.

Screaming. Lots of it. He didn't care.

He was enjoying his meal.

Kevin saw the leader of the enemy fighters run screaming towards George, a different weapon in hand. It resembled an axe except shorter and the blade wider, thinner. He raised it up high as he charged forward. George was oblivious to the danger. Most of the fighters had retreated, a few vomiting at the sight of George having his fill. He had to admit, it was pretty gruesome. For some reason, it didn't faze him at all.

Knowing if he attacked the leader with another whirlwind it would also hit George, he did anyway. Right as the leader brought down the axe, George stopping it with one hand inches from head, the whirlwind knocked all three bodies back. George, being heavier and more agile, was able to stop himself from tumbling too far. The leader landed on his back near the damaged hovercraft, the body of his man not far from him.

Before George could regain his composure, the leader along with two others ran to the half-eaten body of his fighter and dragged him back to the hovercraft.

"Retreat!" The leader yelled.

"Get us the fuck outta' here!"

Like a company of rats, the enemy fled into the hovercraft, sealing it shut. The thrusters sputtered for a second then fully engaged, launching the ship forward. It sped past the group, made a one-hundred-and-eighty-degree turn, and headed back from where it came.

"I wasn't done," George said softly as he turned yellow eyes to the group.

"Oh, yes. You were." Kevin nodded towards Seth and his sister.

The sister was still throwing up with Seth holding her hair back.

"She told me I could eat them." George stood and wiped blood from his mouth with a finger then licked it clean. "What did she expect?"

"For you to have a little decorum," Grannalt snapped. "Christ!"

"Christ?" Kevin looked over at him. "You're an alien. Really?"

Grannalt gave him an angry stare.

"Term of expression, you snot."

"Umm, not a child."

"I'm over two centuries old. To me, you are." Grannalt walked back to the vehicle. "Everybody back in." He turned to George. "Use those medical wipes to clean yourself off. We don't need to smell all that blood."

Inside the vehicle, the AI spoke.

"Recalculating time to destination due to delay."

"Oh, now you talk?" Kevin said, shaking his head.

"Assessment of combat odds was unnecessary. Probability of success ninety eight percent. Time to destination on cruise control four hours."

They rode the rest of the way in silence, taking turns on watch while the others slept. The vehicle came to a craggy hill the size of a mountain on the outskirts of a territory with four towns in each direction. They all got out and stared up at the top of the hill. Kevin nodded.

"Oh, he's there. The fact that he didn't throw some crazy storm at us means he's waiting for us this time."

"Does that mean he'll hear us out?" Xander asked.

"Only one way to find out." Seth pulled out the climbing gear stowed in the undercarriage compartment. "Let's go."

His deadpan delivery with expression to match didn't instill confidence. It would take a few days to climb up. No need to use talent energy. Seth's gut told him the Litigator wasn't going to allow anything that could be conceived as an advantage.

DISSIDENCE

Surrounded by the skeletal remains of petrified trees, Roland focus on the base of the hill and grinned. He watched the group lay out climbing gear on the ground and take inventory. Along with that, they would need rations and water. The vehicle was safe for now since no one without access could get in it.

He was a little disappointed that the group wasn't going to try and get to him via their talents. Then again, they weren't stupid enough to risk unnecessary harm. The same went for the other parties en route towards him. If he saw anything resembling an aircraft, it would be smacked down. From the group below he could sense ire and found George staring up at him with a knowing look.

Both Senigrankes wanted to be released eventually from their prison on Earth. Not long after Darnizva was transported away, the pathways were severed. He was certain the galactic guardians had done so to stop humans from traveling off world. With the pathways inaccessible, so was his connection to the Historian, Bryce. They had planned to raze the planet together and let the creators deal with the spoils. Now, he was alone in that venture.

He also knew George had some other agenda for being on Earth. Since the pathway to the planet opened almost a century ago, only three of their kind had come to look at the food offerings. When that crime group of carnivores popped up in an urban American city a while back, the government assumed it was Senigrankes. Roland felt his disgust resurge at the thought of those heathens.

More movement to the right, brought him out of his reminiscence. On the other side of the hill a unit of New Order soldiers were making their way to the base. By the direction they were taking, running into the group was inevitable. Roland leaned back propped up on his hands and pondered if he should intervene. He noticed the New Order had cannons modified to withstand extreme pressure.

Aww. They thought of me.

It would do no good. He felt they hadn't done their homework well. They were underestimating him. Was he indestructible? By no means. His defenses were. Their cannons were design for battle with known enemies. He had the power of the entire planet at his fingertips. Roland hung his head and sighed.

Even though he didn't want to entertain any of them, he had a soft spot for the group that included George and Kevin. He admired their tenacity whereas the New Order solidified his case against humanity. With that thought, he decided to watch the events unfold and see who would come out victorious.

A shudder ran down Kevin's spine, so he turned to look up at the top of the hill. An afterimage of pale green eyes flashed before it. He leaned against a petrified tree and let his arms hang loose at his sides. Taking a deep breath, he calmed himself.

The Litigator was toying with him again. George came and slapped him on the shoulder.

"If you let him get to you at this juncture, we don't have a chance in hell."

"What's his deal? This isn't his home world. Why does he think he has the right to cast judgement?"

"He doesn't." George saw Kevin frown. "He just wants to destroy humanity because he can."

"Well, that's not right," Erin said. She knelt by a pile of supplies and began sorting them. "He should go back to his planet."

Kevin eyed George and pushed off the tree.

"Why are you still here? You could open a pathway to anywhere and have an all you can eat buffet across the galaxy."

George gave him a sly smile.

"Hmm? I like it here. And I have something else to finish."

"And what's that?"

"I wonder." George tilted his head then walked away.

Grannalt's gaze followed him. The two aliens were hiding something. Kevin could feel it. When he caught Grannalt's stare, the Karysilan looked away and went back to his task.

"What the hell was that about?" He said under his breath.

To his surprise, Seth was next to him.

"Even I know what their thinking." Seth gave him a bewildered look that turned to pity. "Never mind. You're probably better off."

Kevin opened his mouth to protest then stopped himself.

Am I being dumb?

He shrugged it off and went back to help with the gear. The thought of the Litigator watching in gleeful anticipation for their failure still pissed him off. His senses seemed to heighten, and he was able to hear and see farther than normal. From the North, he detected a large number of bodies moving towards their location. The nearly inaudible hum of engines came through his ears loud and clear. Grannalt, Seth and his sister also perked up, looking in the same direction.

"Are you shitting me?" Kevin scratched the side of his mouth, yawning. "Looks like we get to meet the New Order sooner than planned."

⌒

Six combat transports equipped with modified cannons surrounded by a slew of fighter vehicles moved along the terrain in a tight formation. The commanding officer stood at the helm of the lead transport keeping his focus on the barren hill ahead. He clasped his hands behind his back and nodded. The distance meter counted down on the viewscreen.

In a few hours, two of the transports would veer off to form an arch that would be surround the base of the hill on one side. He figured hitting the Litigator all at once would do the job. The creature was not invincible. Served him right for meddling in human affairs.

Why don't you go back to where you came from?

An officer came onto the bridge and stopped a few feet from him.

"Reporting, sir."

"What is it?"

"Detecting a small group of individuals at the base of the hill directly in our path up ahead. Signatures suggest multiple races."

"Time until we reach them?"

"About four hours."

"This is good. We can get a gauge on what the aliens

on this planet intend to do." He pivoted towards his communications officer. "Send word to the second unit. I want a full combat scout team sent ahead for capture or neutralization of that group."

"As ordered, sir." The communications officer touched a few icons on his console. "Link established. Sending instructions."

"I'd hate to use one of our cannon rounds for such a small group but if they prove to be hard to kill, so be it." The commander saw scout teams from the flanking combat units speed out of the hangars. "Good hunting, soldiers," he saluted them.

The enemy was getting close so Xander opened the vehicle and sat in the front seat. He tapped the display screen.

"Calculate enemy assessment and our success rate, please."

The AI came online. Her systems went through the data it was receiving and the screen turned orange.

"Medium threat assessment. Unknown scenarios, success rate is sixty percent."

"Those odds sound sketchy," Kevin said as he approached the vehicle.

"They do have weapons," Xander replied.

"He's coming," Seth announced.

"Who?" Kevin and Xander asked in unison.

An electronic cackle filled the air followed by the sound of someone clearing their throat.

"This area is now under the jurisdiction of the New Order. Surrender yourselves and all weapons, including property and we will ensure your safety."

They all balked at the outrageous request.

"Safety from what?" Kevin called out.

There was a pause before the person answered.

"This hillside is to be bombarded to eradicate a problem in the ecosystem. All surrounding areas will be susceptible to the blasts."

Xander got out of the vehicle and let it seal shut. Kevin smirked at the approaching enemy combat ships.

"Nah, we'll be fine. But you should turn back. It's not safe for you either." Kevin's eyes started to glow. "We don't like being saved by bureaucrats."

"Here he comes." Seth said.

Right as the others in the group turned to question him, a blur appeared before them. Kevin managed to dodge in time by jumping to the side. A thin cut on his arm began to show. Grannalt was able to block the assailant and push them back where they came. The enemy skidded to a stop and with arms raised in a blocking stance, he glared at them.

"Brody." Seth breathed.

Taller, more muscular and fair skinned, the young man resembled Grannalt. He was dressed like an Edo period ninja except for the tight body suit underneath. His face was half hidden behind a dark scarf wrapped around his neck. Grannalt became livid.

"What are you doing with those people?"

Brody's eyes narrowed.

"Those people? They raised me so I kill for them."

Grannalt went pale. Then he frowned.

"That's not what they did! You weren't raised. You were trained to be a monster." Grannalt seemed to plead with him. "Don't you know who I am?"

"Yeah." Brody dropped his arms and went into a fighting stance. "I know who you are." He twirled the blades in his hands and positioned them straight on. "Mother."

Grannalt barely had time to stop his firstborn's blades from piercing his chest. His son relentlessly attacked while the other New Order fighters surged forward, spreading out to take on the others in the group. Even as he held Brody at bay, he could tell something was wrong with Kevin. He seemed unable to muster enough energy to force the horde back. Instead, he relied on his combat training.

"Pay attention to me!" Brody screamed.

One of the blades grazed across the side of Grannalt's forehead. Searing pain exploded in his temple and he staggered back. Brody grinned, brandishing the blade. It had a blue tint. Grannalt slapped a hand on his wound and pressed hard.

"Like that? It enhances pain three-fold. Incapacitates my enemy."

Grannalt regained his stance in time to see his son leap forward for a second blow.

The afterimage of a leg came sweeping towards his son's chest and sent him flying. As Brody landed, Seth appeared standing over him. Before Seth could kick him again, he was up and going for Grannalt. This time, he was chopped in the back of the head by Erin, forcing him to drop to the ground. Dazed by the sudden attack, he clambered up from his knees to return the favor. Seth was on him in a flash and punched him back down.

Without hesitation, Seth began pummeling him in the face and chest. Not letting him get more than a few jabs, even when he managed to rise off the ground for a split second. Seth hit him harder than the last few times but nothing like Erin who came between them, snapping his older brother's head back with one blow. He went still, eyes rolled up in his sockets as he fell.

Grabbing hold of his brother's scarf at the collar, Seth dragged him off to the edge of the woods away from the fighting. There was no emotion conveyed on his face. Grannalt felt disturbed by it. Erin came up and laid a hand on his shoulder.

"No need to worry. Trust me, he's pissed."

Seeing their prized fighter taken out so soon, the advanced New Order team formed a perimeter to block the group from leaving.

George looked up from the attackers he had beaten to submission and squinted at the horizon. Then his expression turned to shock.

"Those stupid fuckers." Kevin gave him a puzzled stare. George pointed. "That."

Kevin saw splotches of white along the left side of the hill's base. Glowing blue orbs from cannon irises grew brighter as they moved into targeting positions. Each one was aimed at the top where the Litigator waited.

"This was just a side project so we wouldn't interfere?" Kevin yelled.

"Proximity danger." The vehicle AI spoke. "Please return to the vehicle and prepare for impact. We are within blast radius of multiple cannons."

"Damn it!" Kevin made quick work of the soldiers in their way. "This is stupid."

The group managed to get clear of the New Order team right before a retreat was called. The enemy rushed back to their vehicles for safety. Xander was the first at the vehicle and opened the hatch for them to get in. The moment the doors sealed them in, they watched the cannons fire. Wide blue beams traveled to the top of the hill. Kevin shielded his eyes, knowing what was to come.

A pale green light shot out from above and engulfed the entire area, blinding everyone in range.

Xander forced his eyes open and winced at the glaring sparkles of light floating outside. The tint shield for the front view panel was not up. He looked down at the panels and found them dark. Tapping on the console didn't do anything. In a panic, he ran his fingers along every instrument, encountering the same.

"No, no, no! What's happening?"

Grannalt stirred from being knocked unconscious by the blast and rolled his head towards Xander. Seeing Xander in a state of despair startled him and he rose quickly.

"What's going on?"

"The vehicle. It's dead." Xander continued trying to push buttons.

Grannalt leaned forward and scanned the wilderness. Nothing moved. As if everything was in the eye of a storm where all was still. Someone kicked the side door hard. Grannalt turned to see Kevin turned longways across the middle seat violently kicking the door until the seal released. It opened two inches, enough for him to pry it all the way with his hands. The look on Kevin's face made Grannalt sit back.

Kevin stomped out onto the packed down dirt and yelled in the air.

"Ahh!"

His eyes glowed followed by a wind turbulence. The stillness dissolve and everything started to move again. Sound filtered back in. The first thing they all heard were New Order soldiers yelling.

"Looks like their stuff is all dead too." Erin struggled out of her seat. "What was that? An EMP or something?"

"Seems so." George got out and stretched his whole body, arms raised to the sky. "It won't last though. Kevin here has disrupted the flow."

"Huh?"

Kevin glanced over his shoulder, his face angry.

As confirmation, the vehicle's dash lit up and all the screens came online.

"System experienced involuntary shutdown. Running diagnostics."

There were cheers echoing from the far regions of the forest. The pale light receded at the top of the hill, allowing the setting sun to reappear. Wheels crunching on the ground caught the group's attention and they saw the advanced team units retreating.

"Now what?" Xander asked.

Kevin stared up at the hill. Seth came out of the vehicle and began gathering up their climbing gear. He stopped for a moment and also looked up.

"We climb."

The New Order combat commander felt humiliated and relieved all at once. The fact that the cannons were essentially useless meant their calculations were wrong. Seeing all the equipment go dead put everyone in a panic. Now back in service, he realized the Litigator was not going to let them destroy him as planned. The commander had a second option. It would take a few days but they had time.

He was certain the Litigator was not going to send another attack unprovoked. Those pesky ingrates on the other side were no longer of consequence. They could be dealt with afterwards. To be on the safe side, he went to his Ops officer.

"Get me a visual on that rogue group. I want to know what they're up to."

"On it, sir." The vidscreen pinpointed their location and zoomed in. "Looks like they're getting ready for a long hike up the hill."

"What the hell for?"

"If I may be frank, sir." His second in command came by his side. "I think they may have the same agenda. It's no secret many factions are sending their best to negotiate with this creature."

"Negotiate! That thing needs to either get off our planet or be destroyed. We have no reason to beg for survival on its whim."

"I agree. That said, I believe that is what's going on."

"Well, we'll just have to beat them to it. Get the gear ready. And prepare detonator capsules. We're taking our weapons of mass destruction straight to him."

"As you command." His second in command turned to the communications officer. "You heard the man. Send the orders to every ship. The faster we get on our way, the better."

"Yes, sir."

The commander smirked. It was a good day for a battle prep.

⤳

Fravral sat in the cockpit of his ship and stared at the pale green light receding. When it showed up, spreading like a disease across the region, he did an emergency stop of the ship. Gragor immediately shut down the engines and Bree cut off all equipment. The signature coming from that light told them what it was. To think the Litigator would use the planet's natural magnetic field to create such a massive EMP type of attack made them nervous. This was no fledgling Litigator.

Such power.

"What do you think happened over there?" Fravral adjusted himself in his seat.

"You mean where we're also going? Did you not see the blue beams before that?"

"Well, yes, I did. Which is why I don't understand. Those weapons would do nothing except piss him off. They need to do better than that."

"They underestimated him." Bree hit the power icon and the panels lit up. "There's another one in that region."

Gragor initialized the engines. When the gauge read full power, Fravral engaged the navigation system and hit the accelerator. The ship rose up from the ground and cruised forward. They observed the landscape and kept silent about their own assessments. Nothing but barren land with clusters of dead trees and bushes, most of it petrified like everything else. They knew of a few territories with greenhouses. The problem was when they tried to put them in the black soil. The plants died within hours despite the water being better than the previous years.

"This is a failure on everyone's part," Gragor stated.

"I'm not sure what caused all this. The general did fire on the planet, but it shouldn't have done this much damage." Fravral maneuvered the ship over a patch of giant trees whose spiky bare tops would cause damage if the bottom hull scraped across them. "The red mist that followed decimated everything in its path."

"How long until we reach the base of that hill?" Gragor asked.

"At cruise speed and stopping for a rest, about eight hours. So, sometime after midnight tomorrow. Unless you're in a hurry, we can ignite the thrusters."

"No. Let's enjoy this for now."

"I hope you don't mean the scenery." Bree didn't look from his station as he said it.

Fravral set the ship on autopilot and relaxed in his seat. Gragor continued to look out the viewscreen at the terrain below.

On approach of the hill's base, Gragor saw multiple movements on the ground.

"Bree, Zoom in."

The viewscreen on the right zeroed in to show a New Order team scrambling around wearing different gear. Farther up the path in a clearing was a lone white vehicle with a small group of people. Gragor sat back in surprise at seeing George.

"I'll be damned." He muttered to himself.

"I'll say," Fravral added in disgust. "That's the group with those kids and the Karysilan."

"Is that right?" Gragor smiled. "This is advantageous."

"How so?"

"Coordinated operations work best." Bree swiveled in his seat, "plus, they have a full blood Senigranke and what seems to be a novice Litigator. We can work with that."

"Wish we didn't" Fravral mumbled under his breath.

"Set us down near them."

As they passed over the New Order team, the operatives stopped their tasks to stare at the ship in awe. Gragor understood why. All the ships in service were capable of flight yet no one dared to use that feature. Even Fravral had kept his ship at a certain altitude to prevent chaos. When the ship hovered over an empty spot in the clearing next to George's group, Gragor saw George staring at the cockpit, one hand over his eyes to block the front lights piercing the predawn.

Landing complete, Gragor cut the engines and went to open the ramp. It slowly settled on the ground and he walked down to greet George. Bree was right behind him with Fravral reluctantly at the rear.

"George. It's been a long time." They stood a few feet from each other. "I see you have a few friends with you."

"Hmph. Not sure that's what we are yet."

Gragor caught Grannalt's gaze and the Karysilan dropped his gear on the ground in anger. They didn't speak for a while, making the rest of the group uncomfortable.

"I am not the enemy anymore. You, of all people, should know that."

"Still doesn't change the fact that we were chased down and your general created this mess." Grannalt stepped over his gear and confronted Gragor. "Did you really try to persuade him to back off? Or did you see some sort of comic relief to engage in?"

"That's not fair, Grannalt!" Gragor met his glare with his own. "You wouldn't have defied your general right off the bat either."

"Let's play nice, shall we?" George suggested.

"Let's not!" Erin came from behind the vehicle and stared down Fravral. "He hurt us over some stupid piece of equipment."

Fravral frowned and moved away from her towards Bree who gave him a disapproving look. Gragor's shoulders hunched and he turned to the girl.

"Yet, here you are, all better." She seemed unsatisfied but walked off. Gragor brought his attention to the rest of the the group. "How about we get to know each other better? I believe we have the same goal." He nodded his head towards the top of the hill.

"He's a stubborn ass," George said.

"Oh, we saw that light spectacle. He's not being cooperative."

Xander extended a hand to Gragor.

"I am Xander Headland. This is my vehicle. I come from Mecca."

Gragor took his hand and held it for a bit.

"Are you not angry at your mother for how you were born?"

Xander shrugged.

"I'm alive. And she regrets that chapter in her life. But, she doesn't regret having me."

"Fair enough."

Grannalt took a deep breath and gestured to the young ones.

"That is my son Seth and my daughter, Erin. My firstborn, Brody, was being an idiot fighting for the New Order, so we had to take him out. He's unconscious in the back of the vehicle."

"Tough love?" Bree quipped.

"And you?" Gragor found Kevin nonresponsive, avoiding engagement with everyone. "Is there a reason you don't wish to introduce yourself to us?"

"Kevin Lang."

Gragor's eyes widened at the name. He glanced over at George, who gave him an amused side stare. He had heard rumors about Professor Morandi's pet assistant. A hybrid with a strange talent that could manipulate weather. There were others who had that talent but his manifested differently. Now, he understood why. A child Litigator. Which was not possible for that race since one had to evolve over fifty to a hundred years to get to such a level.

Is it because he's a hybrid?

Then there was the other question. He tilted his head at George who shook his head and turned away.

So, we're not opening that box?

"So, what's the plan?"

"Up." Seth went back to setting up the gear.

Bree glanced over at the hill.

"It would take a few days. The sides are treacherous."

"Slow and steady." Xander said.

The pod in the rear of Fravral's ship opened and the Cybok came out, hair whipping around him in the breeze. His eyes zeroed in on Seth and the young man stiffened, sensing the probe. Fravral slapped a hand over his face, barring his teeth. Bree's lips pursed and a crooked smile formed as he gave the Cybok a look of pity.

"Good, he's up and about. We need him." Gragor turned back to the ship. "Let's get our own gear ready. I have a feeling we need to get to Roland before those New Order clowns do."

"Why?" Erin asked, confused.

"Because," Bree answered while walking away to follow Gragor. "We don't want to see mass human slaughter."

"It's their own fault if that happens." She said angrily. "They should have left him alone or tried to do what we are. Talk to him."

DESPERATE MEASURES

It took some delicate planning on her assistant's part to weed out the traitor amongst them. The man had no idea he was caught in a spider's web until it was too late. In a dead end hallway he stopped running from the guards in pursuit and turned to face then.

"What are you going to do? Lock me away? Torture me? The New Order will tear this place apart. Then what?"

Alicia came from behind the guards, taking her glasses off and placing them in her lab coat's front pocket. She rushed towards him with inhuman speed, pinning him to the wall. His body was lifted inches off the floor, and he looked into hateful, icy eyes.

"The New Order will not be taking Mecca." Her grin made his blood feel cold. "As for what I'm going to do with you. Torture, like you've never experienced. Don't worry. I won't let you die on me."

She flung him over her head to the floor. A small cracking sound was heard, and the traitor howled in pain. When she turned around, she saw how he landed sideways on his arm. It was definitely broken.

"Medical," the traitor managed to get out. "I need to get to medical."

"Take him to my lab and strap him in. I'll be there shortly."

The traitor's face changed from pain to horror. He was snatched up by the guards and hauled off back to where he came in at. Alicia followed. When they reached her lab and he was secured in one of the triage chairs, the guards left the two alone.

She pulled off her lab coat and took the hairpin out, letting her hair flow freely down her back. She climbed over him and took hold of his arm. He started to scream. She clamped a hand over his mouth.

"First, we fix this. Then we'll move on to the real fun." She whispered in his ear while straddling him so he couldn't move. "Let's enjoy our time together."

The loud snap of his arm being straightened echoed in the room followed by the muffled screams.

Four guards came into Veronica's office and halted in the middle of the room.

"We have a report from Dr. Stern." The leader of the group said.

Veronica looked up from the vidscreen on her desk and swiveled in her chair to face them. Her hair twisted around one side of her neck.

"Go on."

"The traitor has been secured and receiving medical treatment in her lab."

She did a sharp intake through her nose with lips pressed thin, forcing her chest to rise, straightening her posture. She exhaled slowly, feeling relaxed.

"Thank you. Make sure no one goes near that hallway. She will contact us when she's done interrogating him."

"Of course, Professor."

They turned in unison towards the door and exited.

Veronica went back to her screen. She had been trying to place a call via communication links from before the war. On the fourteenth one a connection was established. She took another sharp breath in surprise then brought the image up so that she would be face to face with whoever came on screen.

The facilitator's grim face appeared. He was none too happy to see her. His grey hair that only peppered his temples before was now all over. Yet, he seemed to have not aged.

"Headland." His tone full of disdain, he leaned back in his seat. "Why have you tapped into this channel?"

"You know why! Don't play dumb! Mecca needs help."

"That's a shame. I'm sure you'll figure it out."

"We were to keep in contact. Are you reneging on that part of the bargain?" That made the facilitator angry. She held back her own anger and sat straight. "We had a hunch, long before this, that some of us in the human race would go off the rails."

"Yes. And there was no plan to stop them since our facilities were immune."

"We are not immune!" Veronica slammed a fist down. "Will you help us or not?"

A second feed interrupted follow by another screen appearing next to the facilitator. Dr. Lillian Shriever stood in front of a lab, her face conveying exasperation.

"She is correct."

The facilitator seemed to rear back from his screen. "What is…"

"Oh, this," Lillian tapped the scar on her face. "I wear it with pride. My facility is gone. Destroyed. And the New Order came knocking at Facility Three, where I now reside."

"Impossible!"

The facilitator regained his senses.

"These compounds are resistant to penetration. We made them…" He stopped short as both Veronica and Lillian gave him disgusted looks.

"We're good on our end," Lillian said. "You need to send someone to Mecca."

The facilitator huffed like a child before he answered.

"Very well. I will see who I can get in touch with from our end. Most of those commlinks are broken. We have to do a manual search."

"Thank you." Veronica watched the facilitator's feed wink out. Lillian remained. "How did you connect to this channel?"

"Oh, we saw a long list of feeds being pinged with no response. Figured it had to be another facility. Who else would have those codes?"

"We caught a traitor." Veronica delivered deadpan. "He was giving the New Order our access codes and schematics of Mecca."

Lillian's mouth downturned, her glare intensified.

"Get anything out of them yet?"

"My assistant is working on it."

Lillian snorted.

"I bet she is. Stay safe and hold out as long as you can."

"Why do you say that?" Veronica became wary.

"From our intel, a New Order battalion will reach you by tomorrow. The earliest for their reinforcements is thirty-six hours."

Veronica leaned over her desk with fist clenched on its top while her eyes nearly closed shut as she bared her teeth.

Lillian let out a sigh.

"You just need to keep them at bay for about twelve hours. You have the resources to do at least that much."

"That's not the point!"

"I understand." Lillian's expression turned to sadness. "Do what needs to be done."

The feed cut out and Lillian was gone. Veronica lifted herself off the desk and sat back in her chair. She had not activated the mapping system in a long time and knew it would take a couple of hours to establish a real time grid of the surrounding area. To find the Litigator only took matching his signature from previous data. She touched a commlink icon on the virtual screen of her desk.

"This is Professor Headland. I need all GPS systems online immediately."

A woman's voice came over the feed.

"Is this because of the rumors? Are we about to be under attack?"

No need sugarcoating it now.

"That is correct. A rogue faction of humans called the New Order are attacking facilities to take over resources and communications. We cannot let them through."

"Then we need to know exactly where they are coming from." The woman paused. "Systems will start mapping in ten minutes. Estimated time to completion, one hour four minutes."

"That will do. Thank you."

She disconnected the feed and stared at the other icon on the left side of the screen. Once she activated it, her soldiers would scramble for combat.

Is it too soon?

Shaking her head to clear that thought, she tapped the icon. Lillian's face as she told of her facility's destruction and Facility Three being attacked filled her head.

By morning, Mecca was on lock down. Guards were positioned at every corner, top to bottom. The mapping of the region was complete and the vidscreen above her desk showed a live feed of the New Order making their way towards the facility. From the reports, it had roughly fifty mobile units fully armed and ready to blast through the shields.

A commotion outside her office made her glance over her shoulder at the door. Caleb and Christine came bursting in followed by guards yelling for them to stop. She raised a hand signaling the guards to back off. They stayed in the doorway. Caleb came up to her with his sister in tow.

"We were not assigned deployment orders. Why is that?" His fury filled the room.

"There is no need for you to…"

"This is our home too!" Christine interrupted. "We are trained in combat like the others."

Her son's face contorted.

"Xander can fight for you but we're not worthy? Is that it?"

Veronica stood and ran her fingers through her hair then down the sides of her face. She stared at them with impatience. Their gaze didn't waver.

"Fine. Protect the atrium. It is visible from the outside. Regardless that it's on the tenth level, the New Order has cannons capable of reaching it." Her eyes narrowed. "Can you do that for Mecca?"

"On it."

Caleb grabbed hold of his sister and they pushed their way out the door past the guards.

Alicia arrived and saw them head down the corridor.

"Was that a good idea?" She adjusted her glasses. "They seem a bit too gung ho."

"It gives them a chance to let off steam." She gave a lopsided smile. "What are the chances of that scenario I just made up happening?"

"Oh," Alicia replied playfully. "About ninety percent." Veronica went pale. Alicia laughed. "Like they said, they're combat trained. I wouldn't worry too much."

"Incoming!"

The announcement over the facility commlink boomed. Veronica and Alicia looked up at the live feed of the enemy and saw the glowing cannon of the front unit let off a volley.

"From that far away!" Veronica was livid. "Those sons of bitches!"

"No need to get up close and personal when you can decimate the enemy at a distance." Alicia leaned against the desk with one hand planted on its edge. "Tactics 101."

The shield shook violently from the assault yet held steady. Veronica smirked.

It would take more than that!

As an answer to her dare, six of the ten mobile units' cannons glowed.

"Oh shit!"

The six cannon fire rounds hit the shield protecting Mecca from the outside world and formed a crack that spider webbed out. A second round was imminent and would break through, hitting the side of the main building where the atrium was located.

"Get down!" Alicia tackled her right as the blast burst through the shield creating a gaping hole within the crack. As they landed on the floor, she tapped the commlink in her ear. "Send damage reports to my tablet! Reinforce that shield, now!"

While a secondary shield system that acted as a pinpoint covered the hole, the enemy sent another volley of cannon fire in a separate direction.

"At this rate, the shield will be full of holes and no longer functional."

Both women belly crawled to the destroyed doorway. They could see the trajectory of the cannon blast by the damage in its wake. Once they reached what was left of the corridor, they saw the guards dangling from a hole in the floor. They pulled themselves up and all four stared down at the diagonal path cleared out all the way to the atrium level.

Veronica balled her hands and yelled in a rage. Alicia glanced over at her.

"That's not going to do anyone any good, boss." When Veronica turned that vicious stare her way, she shrugged with her hands up. "Do you. Don't mind me."

"How long before help gets here?"

"Do we really need it?" Alicia cocked her head. "We have soldiers with talent."

"Against that?" Veronica spat, pointing in the enemy's direction. "We're not that kind of facility. This isn't…" she struggled to continue.

Alicia laid a hand on her back, feeling Veronica shudder.

"I get it. Calm down. ETA five hours. We got this."

Approaching Mecca, the Facility sanctioned assistance fighters aligned themselves in an arch and assessed the situation. In the first unit on the command deck Professor Heines stood in the center looking out the viewscreen. He shook his head in disgust. When his group had encountered the New Order in its infancy, they made the decision to steer clear. Over the past few years, he had seen them get bolder in their attacks.

"Looks like Mecca is taking a beating. Shields are at forty percent." The officer at the helm gave his report in a rushed voice. "We will be on them in about an hour."

Professor Heines nodded. He had never thought of himself as a combat leader. The ways of the New World forced his hand. The live feed had shown the first attack and he commended the enemy on their long-range strategy. They knew there was no way of getting into Mecca without disabling the shields. Hours into the fight and it was still up; barely. Enemy forces had infiltrated through the first breech.

"When we get in closer, target the mobile units in the rear. They seem to be doing the most damage."

"Roger that."

Heines let out a tiny 'hmph' and smiled. His group was now nearly two hundred in personnel with a combat unit supplied by the Facilitator. As much as he despised that man, he had to thank him for rescuing his small community when things turned for the worse.

"Hang in there Veronica."

Veronica's son and daughter spread out to each side of the atrium's broken floor to ceiling viewports. They could see the enemy fighters catapult themselves towards them.

"We can't cut them all down," he quipped.

His sister turned to the guards behind them.

"Target as many as you can coming in first. We will handle the ones in the rear."

"Got it!"

The guards pulled out their automatic rifles and knelt in a row. The power indicators by the scopes lit up halfway then they fired. The first enemies to reach the outer wall of the atrium were knocked out of the sky. They fell to their doom as a second group swooped in after. A handful got through the guards' barrage of rounds and the two siblings engaged, rushing them from both sides.

The holoscreen confirmed what Hoskins had known would happen. The New Order had not backed off on the idea of attacking Mecca. He snorted and leaned over the command center's raised platform railing. Those so-called leaders didn't listen to a damn thing he said. They figured Headland would throw a hand across her brow like a damsel in distress and surrender. He knew better.

I'll show them how it's supposed to go.

Up ahead was Metropolis with its top section exposed due to the receded ocean levels. The once pristine white tower was covered in dark blemishes from being battered by the elements. On the frontlines of his combat forces were the New Order soldiers he captured earlier. As promised, he made sure their equipment was up to par. He needed them to break through for him. The less talent he had to encounter, the more he could focus on getting straight to Metropolis' core.

And Terence. He was certain that's where the former Terror resided. Hoskins' mobile unit was in the middle of the formation. This way he was protected on all sides.

"Take one of our units around to the hidden side. I don't want them thinking they can get out any kind of way."

"And the front?" His helmsman asked.

"We're going to form a blockade around it." Hoskins glared at the behemoth through the viewport. "Target the lower level. Let's see how much water it can take in before it floods out."

Come out and play you dirty piece of shit! He challenged Terence inwardly.

Silent alarms accompanied by purple lights went off throughout Metropolis' command center. West looked up from his console with eyes narrowed in hostility. He watched the live feed from outside and saw the large group of combat forces coming towards the compound. Terence came out of the lift and half stumbled to the console. Her murderous gaze landed on the viewscreen. Through gritted teeth, she managed to let out one name.

"Hoskins!"

She had heard his challenge.

The first combat ship moved into position directly in line with the main face of Metropolis. Terence watched the cannon adjust downward and glow. Before West or she could relay an order, the cannon fired. It hit the section right above where the rest sat underwater. The command center shuddered from the impact. A gaping hole began sucking water into the compound.

"Evacuate the sector and seal the outer corridors!" West ordered.

Technicians on the floor, went to their stations. A second round hit the other side of Metropolis. Terence averted her gaze from the main screen to the one on the left. The living quarters' sector right below them was in the same area as the blast. The structure held though dented. She knew another cannon round was coming and it would breach the walls. When it hit, debris flew into the command center, knocking technicians out of their stations. Terence stood against the main console, bent over bracing the gusts, her hair whipping forward to cover her face. She turned around as it died out to see the damage.

A diagonal upwards path nearly two miles long was opened straight to the outside. Pieces of structure dangled along its edges. The artificial landscape that started the Southern Lands territory inside Metropolis was scorched. A mobile combat ship hovered into view. West turned a vicious gaze on her.

"What are you doing?"

Terence walked away into the carnage.

Her eyes glowed purple, electricity sparking around her entire body. With hands clenched tight, she bore the excruciating pain of using talent she had not tapped into for over a decade. Her body tried to revolt but she forced it to endure. She got to the entry of the blast and looked up.

Hoskins was having a laugh at the state of Metropolis on the verge of being riddled with holes by his forces. He sent troops into the open wounds and he could already hear the fighting underway. Which made him frown. There shouldn't have been too much resistance. The answer to his impending question came into view. Transport operators were holding the line inside one of the exposed sectors, pushing his troops back out the compound. Their purple eyes and equipment were lit up with intensity as they moved as one in a single row across the area.

"Ready the cannons. Get rid of those damn things." When his weapons officer didn't answer, he turned to him. "Did you not hear me?" He yelled angrily.

The officer pointed up at the other side of Metropolis. Hoskins followed its path and his eyes widened.

From the ruined sector came Terence rising above Metropolis like an electrified angel. The blue and white static shifted around her, billowing the robe she wore to reveal fair skinned legs. Her glowing stare landed on him and grew brighter.

"There you are." Hoskins sneered.

Seeing Terence in female form made him queasy. He found nothing appealing about her.

"What now, sir?"

The weapons officer shifted uneasily in his seat.

Hoskins knew why his men were suddenly nervous. Many of them had seen Terence in action back in the days of the Terror operations. They were all within range of her attack. He then thought about the situation logically. Metropolis was Terence's baby, created from the ground up under Terence's direct input.

"Keep firing and advance deeper in. Kill anyone in the way." He saw the skepticism on his men's faces. "There's no way Terence would unleash that shit on his own creation. It wouldn't just wipe out all of us but everything that thing's built." His eyes squinted as he smiled up at the image of Terence hovering above. "Checkmate."

He walked over to the hatch and hit the release button. It opened to the sounds of battle. Hoskins grabbed one of the high powered rifled off the rack as he exited the ship. He surveyed the area. So far, not one former Terror had come out of the compound. A group of Transport operatives came towards him and he unleashed a continuous stream of rapid fire. Two went down while the other three managed to dodge the assault, allowing him to get closer to opening made by one of his cannon's rounds. He leisurely strolled towards it, not paying Terence any mind until he felt danger. The hairs stood up on the back of his neck.

Looking up, he saw Terence bring her hands together, the electricity forming into a single beam. It shot out from her body and hit the front lines of Hoskins forces. The crews that could fled out of the ships like rats before the blasts turned them to ash. Hoskins stared in awe at the precision. He never knew Terence had that kind of control over her talent. Thinking about it, he realized the government wanted total devastation. There was never any need for Terence to reign in those parameters. He regained his focus on Terence and stepped back. Terence's face contorted full of rage and she dove.

Hoskins didn't have time to raise his weapon. Terence rammed into him, the impact sending them both backwards. Hoskins landed on his back with

Terence atop him. The former Terror raised an arm and Hoskins saw her fist come down into his face. He squeezed his eyes shut, taking the full brunt of the blow. He then blocked his face as a slew of punches came at him. The block wasn't doing much good since Terence seemed to have anticipated it and sent her blows around to the sides of his head. His vision blurred for a bit. A sudden glitch in Terence's electrical field caught his eye and he took advantage, knocking her off. She went sailing back ten feet before recovering.

"Looks like you're out of practice," Hoskins huffed. He stood to face Terence. "Maybe you should have just let yourself be passed around for morale instead of trained as a Terror. You would have been more useful."

He saw her eyes flicker, purple glow dimming. Her hair was drenched in sweat from exertion. The electric field was sporadic, pulsing in and out. Hoskins retrieved his weapon and flicked the cartridge back on to full auto. He aimed it at Terence and fired, waiting to see the diminished Terror pulverized by a stream of rounds.

Terence's body refused to do as she asked. She could feel the intensity wane and her mind screamed for it not to. Please! She just needed one last push. Hoskins' words flooded in and something inside her broke. She remembered the first time she had seen him, pleading for his help. There were other times when he was on the base unaccompanied by his father and watched, laughing, as some of his men beat her down so they could do as they pleased. She had killed them the moment her talent restraint came off for a mission.

That was the start of Terence's revolt. Hoskins' father had already turned the Terror operation over to him so there was no one to blame for letting it get that far except him. Terence looked up at Hoskins and saw the barrage of firepower coming at her. Hoskins' victorious grin was an insult. Rage renewed, a surge of electricity went through her and the rounds were met by an invisible shield. They stopped dead midair and dissolved into nothing.

Hoskins' face scrunched up in frustration and his fingers went to pull the trigger again. His expression turned to surprise. He looked up into Terence's eyes engulfed in purple light. He had not seen her move. His body sizzled from contact with the energy field as he finally felt what was wrong. Her hand was fully inside his chest and going deeper until her wrist was no longer visible. Hot blood gurgled in this throat and came up dark and thick like tar.

No. Not like this. Not by this piece of garbage!

Hoskins brought the rifle up and hit Terence hard in the side of the head. Her head was knocked sideways. She pulled her hand out of his chest and he hit her again, this time sending her to the ground. He had his finger back on the trigger when her fingers came up and sunk into the meat right between his ribcage and under the shoulder. With a twist, she severed his arm from his body. He screamed in horror and pain, stumbling away from her only to fall.

With a viciousness Hoskins had witnessed from his subordinates against enemies on his orders, Terence tore into him in a crazed frenzy. Her eyes seemed to glaze over. Hoskins felt his strength give out along with part of his intestines. The wounds were being cauterized by the electricity, keeping him from dying quickly.

This thing wants me to suffer. He managed a crooked grin. You proved me right. He thought to her. You're all nothing but monsters. I win.

Terence's eyes flickered with pure malice. Her hand went to his face and forming a claw, punched through, tearing the head apart. Cooked blood, still sizzling, splattered on her face as she withdrew before it dried. She sat back straddling what was left of his torso. Staring up at the sky, she let out a loud wail and began crying.

West stood on the edge of the battlefield outside Metropolis and watched Terence fall into despair. He understood. The fight had already dwindled to a few hotspots. When he saw Terence ascend, he felt obligated to head out with an army of his own. Neither side was willing to budge. Seeing Hoskins fall had brought about a desperate advance by some of his high rankers. One fighter unit retreated, leaving the others to fend for themselves. West recognized Jesse climbing onto the retracting ramp of a ship's opened hatch.

You fucking coward.

He raised one arm and using a finger, formed an energy burst that shot up into the sky. Former Terrors emerged from the compound. West smiled as he dropped his arm back down. He wasn't going to give Hoskins the satisfaction of seeing them in action once more. Now that the former general was dead, it was time to clean up.

STALEMATE

"So," Gragor stood with arms folded. "Who's going up there to have it out with that narcissist?"

The rest of the group stopped what they were doing. Seth was bent over about to sling on the backpack full of climbing gear.

"I thought we were all going. This is Xander's personal mission. And we decided to support him."

"That's great and all, but not feasible." Gragor gestured with his head towards the New Order forces. "Don't think for one moment, they won't come back to get rid of us."

Grannalt dropped his gear.

"You're right. Someone has to stay here and hold the fort for the rest of you to come back. I'll guard the vehicle."

"You three," Bree nodded at Xander, George, and Kevin. "You have to go." He turned to Fravral. "I say send the Cybok as a rear guard."

"That sounds about right." Gragor unfolded his arms and stared up at the hill. "It's going to take a while. Don't get hasty."

While the four made their way up the hill, Gragor paced. Fravral sat on the ground next to his ship. Yells echoed through the forest surrounding the hill's base as New Order commanders gave orders to the soldiers climbing up with canisters strapped to their backs. Gragor looked up at the humans obeying. He shook his head in pity. Fravral followed his stare.

"They still haven't learned a damn thing."

Gragor's brow raised.

"Hmm? You sound almost like one of them." Fravral frowned at that. "Let's wait and see how it goes."

By the next day, the four from their group were a third of the way up along with some of the humans. On the second day they were more than halfway. Grannalt was inside the vehicle monitoring Brody hooked up to the medical unit and still unconscious. Seth watched the typography on the display screen while his sister scouted the area with Bree.

In the late afternoon, the group was settled in their makeshift camp. Seth still manned the cockpit of the vehicle in Xander's place.

"Incoming combat ship from Southwest coordinates," the vehicle AI announced.

Seth sat back from the screen in surprise. The others perked up at that. Grannalt climbed to the front and took a look for himself.

"Where's it heading?"

"Time until engagement, less than two hours."

"Can't you pinpoint the exact time?" Gragor asked the AI.

"Ship is accelerating. Weapons are in flux. Full charging likely in progress."

"New Oder reinforcements?" Gragor leaned into the opened hatch and stared at the screen. "How many we talking?"

"Total number of ships, one. Full combat unit equipped with twenty mobiles. Designation Terror Group. Support battalion one zero zero three."

Grannalt and Gragor reared back at the information.

"What does that mean?" Erin asked.

Seth shrugged. Bree and Fravral gave each other confused looks.

"Hoskins," Grannalt and Gragor breathed out.

"What signature is that vessel?" Grannalt demanded.

"Please wait." The AI went silent while it probed. "Signature is identified as Jesse Kane. Cabinet member of the former United States of America."

Gragor saw a hateful expression cover Grannalt's face and he stepped away from the vehicle. He had seen that look before from Hana, the Shadow Organization's head of operations. What happened afterwards was not for the weak. Seeing Grannalt with the same look had him worried. He had heard of Jesse being a spy for Hoskins. A spineless human in his opinion. It was apparent Grannalt's impression was vastly different.

Grannalt had not intented on remembering the horrors he endured at the hands of humans while in captivity. The invocation of those two names; Hoskins and Jesse. That was enough to send his mind in a downward spiral. Hoskins Sr's idea of patriotism was cruel and counterproductive. Jesse's feelings towards aliens was explicit whenever he turned a blind eye to the abuse he witnessed. Grannalt got out of the vehicle and stood in the clearing. He stared at the sky waiting for Jesse's ship to show up.

⸜⸝

After watching Terence go stone crazy and tear his boss apart like a ragdoll, Jesse hauled ass with what he could and headed towards the next phase of Hoskins' plan. For a day and a half, he kept is men and the ship under wraps in case Terence decided to come hunting.

When that didn't happen, he called an all-clear. The coordinates for the Litigator was over five hours away if he went at moderate speed.

It was a couple of hours into their journey that his navigator saw the heat signatures crawling all over the area surrounding the Litigator's location. Jesse had him zoom in and he saw the swarm of New Order vehicles formed in an arch along the base. A separate set of ships were on the opposite side. He made out the Relliant ship and a combat transport.

"Get me all the info. I'm going to make sure the rest of the team is ready to go."

"Yes sir." The navigator turned to his counterpart. "You heard him."

Jesse left the mini bridge of the ship and into the hangar. He talked with the combat leader and they did a weapons check on all the mobile units. An hour went by in no time so he was surprised when the navigator called him through the commlink.

"Got some updates and a better visual."

Jesse excused himself from the combat leader and went back to the bridge.

"What you got?" He leaned forward over the console.

"Not gonna' believe it." Jesse gave him an exasperated stare. "From the archives, I have established the Relliant ship to be of the Command Fleet." Jesse tilted his head to the side in astonishment. "Gets better. The transport vehicle is registered to Mecca."

"You're kidding!"

"Nope. And," the navigator tapped the screen and the image zoomed in more. "It seems this one is waiting for us."

On the screen was Grannalt staring in their direction. Arms relaxed at his side, his eyes said otherwise.

Jesse curbed his urge to spit on the image.

"That fucking test specimen is still alive."

"He looks angry as hell."

"Ready weapons. We take him and those Relliants out first then head to the Litigator before those New Order assholes mess it all up."

He sat in the center command chair fuming.

We couldn't take down Terence but this one I'll make sure to get rid of.

Grannalt waited for the ship to get close enough, not caring if the weapons fired on him or not. He was grabbed by both arms from behind and he started to protest. Gragor dragged him back to the vehicle. Seth managed to get a hold of him as well.

"Have you gone mad?" Gragor yelled.

"Let go!" Grannalt struggled to get out of their grip. "I want to tear that bastard apart!"

"And how are you going to do that if you get hit by a laser cannon and turned into ash?"

Grannalt got free and stumbled back from them. He knew he was being irrational. His hatred for the U.S. Government would not be extinguished. Seth cupped his face in his hands. The two stared into each other's eyes and a sick feeling came over Grannalt. His children had suffered like him and justified in being just as angry. Yet, they were calm. Erin stood silently nearby.

The ship made its approach and let loose a beam of energy that hit the hilltop where Xander, George, the Cybok, and Kevin were located. It made a large gash in the bedrock. Instead of falling, they catapulted themselves further up, avoiding the blast. Bree tsked in disgust and went into Fravral's ship to get one of the handheld cannons.

Kevin turned around using one arm as he dangled from a narrow piece of the edge. He saw the ship and let his eyes zero in on who was visible on the command bridge. Seeing Jesse made his body heat rise. On his right, George was doing the same and had an even worse expression on his face. Xander climbed up onto a bigger ledge and looked down at the camp right as the ship sent cannon fire at it. To his relief, the shot went wide, missing the vehicle and the ship.

The Cybok was already above them, his left arm configuring into a cannon. He targeted the ship and when the strength indicator hit the third level, he fired. The side part of the ship's forward section was blown open, causing it to teeter but not fall. Bree came out of Fravral's ship with the handheld and aimed for the ship's underbelly. The blast knocked the ship upwards and it started to zig zag.

Roland watched with interest as everything combined in one scene. He recognized Jesse as well and found it amusing that the sniveling traitor had grown a pair. Some of the New Order soldiers had made it to the top with their detonators while the group battled it out with the rogue ship. Xander, George, Kevin, and the Cybok emerged from over the edge. The Cybok configured his other arm.

"No, wait!" Xander cried out. The Cybok hesitated. Xander stepped closer to Roland. "We came here to try and make you see reason."

Roland's brow shot up.

"Reason? What for?"

"This is our planet. You need to let us try to fix this on our own."

"But that's the problem," Roland sneered. "You can't. Your kind is not capable of coming together. I saw that first hand in the battle."

George stood next to him with Kevin not far behind.

"You need to let this go. It's the same if our world was in this situation."

Roland's eyes began to change and his power swelled. Taking that as an act of aggression, the Cybok's arms lit up.

"Stop!" Xander yelled.

The cannons fired. And did nothing to Roland as they bounced off the energy shield surrounding him and redirected to the Cybok, knocking him off the hilltop. Xander turned to confront Roland and found the alien's attention was not on them. The swaying ship managed to unleash another blast that sent Xander sailing off the cliff behind the Cybok. George and Kevin tried to reach for him but were unsuccessful.

They caught sight of a few New Order soldiers taking advantage of the situation and planting their detonators. It also got Roland's attention and sent him beyond rage. What appeared to be spears made of wind and cloud formed in the sky spanning most of the hilltop and the valley below. The top section of spears tilted in a thirty-degree angle towards the ship while the rest were pointed straight down. George grabbed Kevin and pushed him down onto the ground, laying atop him. Roland unleashed his deadly assault.

The detonators went off at the same time yet couldn't penetrate the energy field surrounding Roland. The New Order soldiers scrambling to get down were caught in the aftermath of their own bombs. Jesse's ship was knocked out of the sky to Grannalt's waiting hands.

Jesse saw the end coming when the Litigator unleashed his unholy power. He had already evacuated his men. The spears coming straight down were in a perfect circumference that barely missed the camp by a quarter mile. Disappointment consumed him.

Gonna' have to do it myself, then.

The group watched in awe at the spectacle of destruction Roland laid before them. Grannalt followed the wind spears directly above speed towards Jesse's ship. They tore through it, creating mangled holes. Grannalt regained his position, with both vibrating cylinders in his hands, in its flight path. When it got close enough to strike, he brought them up in an X and swung them out. The sonic vibrations carried off into the air and quartered the ship. Right before it exploded, a jumpseat apparatus shot out from its rear. The jet pack sputtered as it engaged lasting a few seconds then failing. Grannalt saw Jesse fumbling with the controls in frustration as it fell to the forest.

"Oh, no you don't," Grannalt sneered. "You don't get to escape."

Bree wasn't fast enough to stop him this time. Grannalt took off in the direction of Jesse's fall. Seth and Erin were ready to follow.

The Cybok landed with a loud thud onto the New Order vehicle sitting less than a quarter mile away. His heavy body caved in the top conforming to his shape. Fravral rushed to him, frantic. Seth hesitated, concern on his face for the Cybok, while his sister decided to continue pursuit of their mother. Bree caught movement in the sky to his right and looked up. Xander was in free fall. He tsked, tossing the gun to the ground and ran to Fravral's ship. He went to the main console and activated the tractor beam. Targeting Xander, he hit the release. Xander stopped with a jerk, suspended in the air. Bree manipulated the controls so that it brought him in slow. He averted his gaze to the hilltop.

From the top down, it was a landslide of murder.

Grannalt made it to the clearing where Jesse would have crashed and found only the apparatus. From the way it was laid on the ground, the thrusters must have engaged at the last moment, making a safe landing. He swirled around, checking the area and barely dodged a beam of laser fire. Jesse came out from the dense petrified trees with a primal yell as he ran towards him firing away. Grannalt deflected the rounds with the cylinders while backing further into the edge of the clearing.

His rounds spent, Jesse tossed the gun aside and plowed into Grannalt, taking him off guard. The two fell to the ground and Jesse managed to get a hold of his neck. He squeezed as hard as he could but Grannalt head butted him, forcing him to loosen his grip. Grannalt brought up one knee and knocked Jesse off him. To his surprise, the man recovered quick and kicked his hands, sending the cylinders flying.

A split second was all Jesse needed. He came at Grannalt and delivered three punches in succession, getting the upper hand. Grannalt took them, not falling from the blows. Jesse went to swing with another and Grannalt ducked down, slamming his fist into Jesse's gut. He doubled over as his body was lifted off the ground and sent sailing into the nearest tree. Grannalt stood and waited for him to come again.

"I see you learned some skills," Grannalt said, wiping his mouth.

Jesse got up and shook his head a few times, tapping the sides with an open palm. He met Grannalt's gaze with an equal amount of rage and hatred.

"You fucking aliens! Just cuz you helped us advance our technology doesn't mean we have to tolerate you."

"Helped you?" Grannalt's eyes brightened. "I was taken against my will!"

"Yeah." Jesse smirked. "We made good use out of

you. A real handy consumable product." He launched himself towards Grannalt.

Grannalt felt his body go numb with a level of rage he had not encountered. Jesse seemed to be coming at him in slow motion even though he knew each attack was much faster. With ease and a sense of disinterest, Grannalt evaded every punch and kick countered with one that landed on Jesse. By the smeared arcs of color that accompanied them, he knew from the outside it appeared the two men were fighting at warp speed. Somehow, Jesse landed another hit, snapping Grannalt out of his serenity. The sharp reality of time came rushing back. He grabbed hold of Jesse's head and slammed it into the ground.

"Did you really think you could match me in hand combat, you shitty human?"

Jesse tried to remove Grannalt's iron grip from squeezing his head in a vice, to no avail. Grannalt lifted his head up and slammed him back down.

"I will never forgive you for what you've done to me!"

With each word, Grannalt brought Jesse up only to drill his head deeper in the hard soil, forming a hole. He straddled the man, letting go of his head and began to punch him. Jesse's body bounced with each strike.

"Stop it!" His daughter's voice was nearby but he paid no heed. "Please, don't do this! He's not worth…"

"You will suffer!" Grannalt yelled at Jesse, tears blinding him.

Arms wrapped around his waist and hands stopped his assault, cupping his own together.

"You can stop now," Seth said softly. "He's already dead."

Grannalt's vision cleared and he saw the bloody mess beneath him. He suddenly saw a glimpse from

Jesse's mind that lingered before his last breath of how Hoskins met his demise. He could clearly see Terence in the same position except from above. Jesse's point of view. Horrified by the images, he stumbled backwards off Jesse and tried to crawl away. Erin held fast to him.

"You don't understand," Grannalt finally cried. He rest his head in his hands. "The things they did to me. That he knew they were doing." He removed his hands and stared at Seth. "And he did nothing!"

"We do know," Erin whispered.

Seth walked over and knelt before him.

"Some connections, no matter how much we want to sever or block them, can't be broken."

Grannalt sat in despair as the implication of what Seth said sunk in. And like Terence, he bawled like a small child, his own children attempting to console him.

〜

Ruined transport ships lay strewn along the base of the hill. New Order soldiers struggled to regain their dignity while attempting to rescue those trapped on its sides. The last attack from the Litigator sent the soldiers scaling upwards with high powered detonators down into the petrified wilderness. Some of them were found impaled on treetops. This was not how the operation was supposed to go.

The commander staggered out of his damaged ship; one arm held against his side. He was sure it was just dislocated although the pain suggested otherwise. His men followed him out and those still able bodied joined the rest in the rescue mission. He stared up at the top of the hill and cursed the Litigator.

You monster! I hope you get what you deserve.

He couldn't see what was going on atop the hill, but he knew Kevin and George were up there ready to take the Litigator to task if necessary. As much as he hated the idea of them taking the New Order's glory, eliminating the Litigator was top priority. A petrified tree cracked at its center and fell onto one of the combat ships, piercing the hull.

This is our planet. We need to fix it ourselves.

A storm brewed around Roland. Kevin and George had recovered from the attack were on their feet. He waited for them to make a move. They seemed hesitant. And he figured out why in an instant. Standing face to face with the hybrid and George he saw the answer to his long-standing mystery. He noticed during their trek across the territories that both had the same stance and gait, yet Kevin had power he shouldn't. Like his own. George gave him that knowing look again.

He remembered them arriving on Earth at the same time. Neither was in their right state of mind, starved from travel and regressed to primal instinct. It was a dark deserted area in an obscure part of what they now know to be Europe. A human female was alone, walking the road. They fought over her, desecrating every inch of flesh while forcing her body to regenerate after each bite. Having their fill, they left her in a field to die.

Here, standing before him was the product of that horrid night. A commingling of the two Senigranke's DNA in a third species. Kevin seemed to realize a similar answer as he stared at him in shock and resentment. Roland could see him counting their resemblance, not knowing that George was part of the equation.

"Why have you come here?" Roland added force to the storm.

Kevin stepped into the pressure and kept his balance.

"You need to listen to reason!"

Kevin had to yell over the howling winds.

"Let the humans have it. Once the pathways are reopened, you can leave." George stood unbothered by the storm. "Stop this farce at negotiations. You never had any intention of being fair."

"True." Roland side stepped, keeping an eye on them. "It was quite entertaining though."

"You won't back down?" Kevin found his center, able to stand against the storm like George. "Then, I guess…" His eyes glowed an icy pale green and wisps of light of the same color formed before him. "I have to stop you myself." He opened his arms, palms up and two swirls of light assembled in his hands. "I've never pushed myself to see what my limit is. Not sure I can handle it. But if I can stop you, then so be it."

A new storm erupted from the sky and pushed down Roland's jet stream. Gravity seemed to increase ten-fold and the hill quaked with fear of crumbling. Roland forced himself to endure the onslaught by planting one foot forward and bending his knees. He could see how much power Kevin was drawing. A dangerous amount that, as he concluded, his body probably couldn't handle.

Kevin envisioned planet Granada, letting his mind go there. It loomed before him and its light enveloped him, giving him a surge of power. A spike in his storm's intensity caused the ground to crack open in a circle around the three men.

Roland saw George make a dash towards Kevin and knew he was not going to reach him in time. Roland broke away from the pressure right as Kevin's body began to lift off the ground. The light was coming out of him from every orifice, every pore. Roland slammed into him, knocking him back down.

"Don't," he punched him in the chest, his body making a dent beneath him as he landed with a heavy smack against the ground, "make me," Kevin tried to get up and Roland hit him again. "Hurt you." Kevin's body sunk deep in the ground. Roland grabbed him by the neck with one hand and they locked eyes. He punched him, then wrapping his hands around his neck, squeezed, blocking off his windpipe until the light dimmed out.

A blow to his side sent him fifty feet away from Kevin.

"Get off." George stood where he once sat with yellow eyes glowing. "Don't touch him."

"What, you're going to protect our child?" Roland spat out blood and touched his side. "He's an anomaly. He shouldn't have such power."

"That's not for you to decide."

Roland pressed on his side.

"You broke something."

"Serves you right. And no, I'm not going to heal you."

"I wouldn't ask you to." Roland turned to him with a sly smile. "He's also mine. I get to have a say in what becomes of him."

Tendrils of dirt rose from the ground and formed sharp tips on their ends. They shot out straight towards Kevin's unconscious body. George pivoted in time to block the attack, the tendrils drilling into his back. He picked up Kevin despite the pain and stood. Roland retracted them, his face expressing disappointment.

"Humans are a disease. That child is half their species. Regardless if he's mine, I can't let him live with these things." He frowned. "No. Because he is also mine, I won't allow it."

The Book of Litigation reformed as Roland stood. With each flip of its pages the connection with the planet made it glow brighter. His body lifted from the ground enveloped in a translucent bubble and light beams shot from his eyes. In a language only Mother Earth could understand, he began to chant his requests.

George fell to one knee and cradled Kevin in his arms. At that moment he wanted to evolve. Just long enough to take Roland down. He started to regret not letting himself absorb all his race's knowledge. With eyes squeeze shut he bowed his head.

Why? How could this happen?

The sky suddenly turned black, darker than night and Roland's power was cut off like a switch. He dropped to the ground in surprise, wincing from pain as he landed flat on his back, then looked up. George opened his eyes and did the same. A white hairline fracture appeared in the sky, growing wider until ethereal light nearly blinded them.

"Stop!"

The voice carried throughout the region echoing down in the desolate valley. A figure in white robes emerged from the crack and floated towards them, stopping above. Chestnut hair flowed around a pale face with luminous blue eyes. Another came beside them, their skin a deep sensuous brown wearing the same robes and golden eyes.

"Litigator," they said in unison. "You are in the wrong."

The double vibration of their voices shook the hillside. Roland stared at them in anger.

"Arenans."

"Did you not think we were observing?" The first asked.

"Of course, I knew. Who else would close the pathways?"

"We wanted you to see the humans' point of view," the pale Arenan said.

"Yet, you refused to look any deeper and get to know them." The other added.

Kevin started to convulse, regaining consciousness. George held him steady until his body stopped. He looked around the carnage on the hilltop and found a freshly dead New Order soldier. While the Arenan's attention was on Roland, George ripped a small piece of flesh from the corpse and carried the dripping tissue back to Kevin. He tore off some of it and went to put it in Kevin's mouth.

Kevin's eyes flew open and he tried to push back from him, shaking his head.

"No. Don't want…" His eyes grew wider. "I won't."

"You need it." George pressed his weight down on him and shoved the bloody remains down Kevin's throat. "Don't fight."

Yet, he did. Kevin's body arched off the ground as the taste permeated every corner of his being. His eyes glowed yellow. George slowly pulled his fingers from Kevin's mouth.

"Ahh!" Kevin whimpered and began to cry. "Please!"

George could see the euphoria take hold. Kevin writhed beneath him then went still. He had fallen unconscious again. His breathing started to regulate. George felt like he was being stared at and turned his head. The Arenans were done talking to Roland for the moment.

They were focused on George.

"You must take care of him. We are sending you back to where he needs to be."

George started to open his mouth in protest and light engulfed him. Kevin and George winked out of existence, leaving Roland with the Arenans.

At the base of the hill, Xander, propped unconscious against the vehicle, disappeared before his party and Gragor's. Bree glanced up at the Arenans daring them to do the same with the Relliants. The pale one caught his eye and the two aliens had a silent standoff. Gragor reached over and pulled Bree away.

"Don't. We have never encountered a guardian like this before. Tread carefully."

The Arenan averted their gaze and gave its attention back to Roland. Bree hissed then obeyed Gragor, walking to Fravral's ship. Grannalt stood stunned and confused. He ran a hand along the hull of the vehicle and breathed a sigh of relief. His firstborn was still unconscious inside.

"Should we?" Grannalt started to ask.

"Stay right where we are until we know what they are up to," Gragor answered angrily. "For all we know, they think we're hostile."

Grannalt nodded and leaned against the vehicle.

"At least we're not stranded."

Fravral was rooted by his ship in awe of the Arenans. His eyes began to burn from staring at their brightness and he finally brought an arm up as a shield. He turned to Bree.

"Their dangerous, aren't they?"

"More than you know." Bree stepped into the ship.

"They look like," Erin said with her lips lopsided, "Angels."

"Those are no angels," Gragor snapped. "Stay quiet and don't do anything that may be interpreted as a threat."

Erin pouted then went into the vehicle. Seth took off in the pod's direction and climbed on top of it at the hatch. Grannalt's eyes went wide with fear.

"What are you…" Fravral started to yell.

Gragor clamped a hand over his mouth.

When it was removed, he projected in a low voice.

"Get away from there!"

Gragor stopped Grannalt mid flash step. The hatch opened. Seth stared down into it for a while then climbed in. Fravral's mouth gaped open as the hatch closed, sealing Seth inside with the Cybok. Gragor pursed his lips and tapped Fravral on the shoulder.

"It's probably better this way."

Inside the pod, Seth laid facing the Cybok, his knees nearly to his chest, and the two stared at each other.

"You don't really want me," Seth whispered. "You just need someone to make you feel better."

Even in the dark, he could see the change in the Cybok's black eyes. The Cybok pulled him closer and closed his eyes. Sadness fell over Seth and he caressed his cheek.

"It's okay. You don't have to fight anymore. There's another out there who will love you. A soul mate all your own."

A low sonic wail echoed in the pod.

"Shh." Seth rested his head against the Cybok's chest and listened to his internal system.

～

Terence dropped the mug of steaming coffee on the command center floor and looked on as a rift opened in the middle of the room. George tumbled out, still holding on to Kevin. The operatives on deck stopped what they were doing and witnessed the phenomenon. They had already gotten over the sky being black with those blaring white fractures a few moments ago.

"What is this?" Terence went over to them. "What's happening?"

George rolled on his side and knelt.

"Your mate decided to test his limits with the Litigator."

"What!" Terence got to Kevin's side and placed a hand on his left pectoral. She closed her eyes and focused on Kevin's heart. When she opened them, she exhaled. "There's no tears in the muscle. He should be fine." Then she turned to George. "How are you with him?"

There was no love lost between the two. Terence knew all about George and despised the American government, especially its leaders.

"Before you go all nuclear on me and cause more damage to this facility, hear me out first." George looked around and saw the way everyone was acting. "Or, you tell me what happened here. I sense a victorious vibe."

Terence's face scrunched up and a gleam formed in her eye. George wasn't sure if that was a good sign.

"Get Kevin to medical," Terence ordered. Two operatives came into the room and hauled him off like a dead body. She turned back to George. "Let's go to one of the conference rooms and I'll tell you all about." As George got up and brushed himself off, Terence noticed the holes in his back. He pointed at them. "Do you need to take care of those wounds first?"

George smirked.

"Not really. It would take more than this to harm me."

"So you say."

Terence walked to the lift. George followed.

You arrogant shit.

Terence smiled and without turning around replied telepathically.

I know.

CHAPTER FIVE

COMPROMISE

Medical technicians tended to Kevin while George sat in the conference room waiting for Terence to come back. She was adamant that Kevin took priority over the other patients much to West's chagrin. The rest of the bloody mass from the downed New Order soldier was in George's pocket. He pulled it out and shoved the whole piece in his mouth. It didn't taste all that great, having gone slightly bad. He only cared about its healing properties. The wounds in his back started to slowly close. More than that was required to fully regenerate.

The door opened and Terence strolled in with a terse expression. Her combat suit hugged every inch of her body. George noticed for the first time how much Terence had changed. She was rounder, less toned, yet still formidable.

"What did you do to him?" Terence sat down two seats away from him and slapped her hands on the table. "His body is in a state of confusion."

"Oh? Must be what I gave him to eat."

Terence leaned away from him in horror.

"You didn't," she breathed.

"It was the only way to get him back to normal."

"Why? You could have left him alone. There was no reason to…"

"Because he's mine."

Terence stared at him in disbelief.

"What?"

"He's my child. I will do what I need to for his sake."

"Holy shit." Terence covered the bottom of her face with both hands. Then her eyes narrowed. "But, he's not a maneater. You can't feed him that!"

"All Senigrankes are carnivores. It so happens many who evolve tend to steer towards lessening their intake."

"So, what happened? How did you end up falling out of the ether into Metropolis?"

"I thought you were going to share first." George gave her a sly smile. Terence lowered her stare. "Alright. We found the Litigator and went to negotiate."

"And?"

"He wasn't in the mood. That's when Kevin tried to out litigate him."

"Why didn't you stop him?"

"Who?"

Terence slammed a fist down on the table.

"Kevin!"

"And how was I to do that? I'm not evolved like them." George took his coat off and tossed it on the chair beside him. "Besides, we have a new problem."

"The sky turned black."

"Yes. The guardians of this part of the galaxy have shown up."

"Guardians?"

"Arenans. Some people have seen them on rare occasions and think they are angels."

"They're not?" The way George's eyes turned a different shade of yellow gave Terence her answer. "What do they want?"

George sat back in his chair, his legs fully extend.

"Your turn."

Terence pursed her lips.

"Fine. Hoskins showed up." She squirmed in her seat. "The battle was fierce."

"You killed him." George stated.

Terence seemed to flinch at his words. Sadness and guilt showed in her demeanor.

"I did."

"Something he said?"

"He," Terence paused. "He said I proved him right. He called me a monster!" Terence spat out angrily. "I'm not…we're not…"

George waited for her hands to stop clenching and unclenching before he responded.

"If you know it's not true, then there's nothing for you to feel ashamed of."

"I know that!"

"Where's his body? Did the retreating forces take it?"

"There wasn't much left to take," Terence whispered.

That caught George off guard and he nearly slid out of his chair in shock.

"What did you do?"

Terence sat silent for a long time. She pushed herself up using the table and stood.

"I think you should rest up. Not sure what's in store for humanity come tomorrow." She headed out of the room and stopped at the doorway. "One of the operatives will show you to a room that's still intact."

George remembered the gaping holes lined with debris. Metropolis had been violated.

∽

White light invaded Kevin's closed eyelids. He squeezed them tight to try and shut it out. That didn't work so he slowly forced his eyes open. The familiar walls of Terence's private chamber came into view. Holoscreens covering the walls flickered through different territories. All around the planet, the sky was black as pitch with ultra-white fractures disrupting the dark.

He sat up on his elbows and gazed up at the feeds before laying back down. Closing his eyes, he took a deep breath. Weight pressed on top of him. He opened them back to see Terence straddling him. She wore a form fitting combat bodysuit that barely contained her curves.

"It seems your thing is to always want to violate me when I'm not conscious."

She frowned, her expression hurtful.

"That's not true."

He ran his hands along her breasts and down to her abdomen.

"Are you going to keep wearing this?"

He took hold of the neckline and ripped the fabric open all the way down to between her thighs, exposing fair skin that hadn't seen the sun in years. Lust consumed him. She stared down at him with disinterest then pulled the fabric together, letting the nanobytes seal it. He reached up to grab her and she smacked his hand away.

"Why are you always so mean to me?" He sighed in defeat.

Terence slid off him to stand at the end of the bed.

"If you're in that good a condition, then get up. We have things to do."

Kevin sat up again and was disappointed to find he was dressed in a tee shirt and scrub pants. He threw the covers off and swung his legs over the side. Terence was in a state of distress. She didn't show it. He could feel it. Standing, he went closer to the wall of holoscreens, blocking her view.

"I heard what he said." Terence tensed up behind him. "Hoskins. What he called you."

"I. What I did to him."

"You're not what he says. You're not a monster. None of us are." He turned to face her. "However he met his end, does not make you one."

"You wouldn't say that," Terence whispers. "If you knew."

Kevin grabbed her face and brought her close to him.

"I don't care. He deserved whatever you gave that bastard."

George sensed the Arenan coming within seconds before their arrival. He turned to Kevin and Terence standing at the main control panel getting updates from West. The light flickered once, throwing the entire room into pitch darkness then white light permeated everything. Both Kevin and Terence tried to use their talents to stop the assault and found they could not.

From the light came an ethereal creature bathed in white. Blonde hair, fair skin, giant white wings and eyes of silver starlight. There was nothing beautiful about those eyes. They conveyed pure disdain. The Arenan left no doubt how he felt about humans.

"Eater, you don't belong here." The Arenan met George's glare. "This planet will be stripped of its species. You should go home."

"How about I just go hunting instead?"

George goaded him while smiling.

Fury filled the Arenan's expression.

"I would rather you didn't. But, if you insist, I will exterminate you now."

Terence pushed forward past George with Kevin attempting to stop her.

"What do you want? We've had enough alien intervention!" Terence had to strain her neck to look up.

"Is that so?" The Arenan spread his arms wide. "And what is this monstrosity you have built with the intervention of another race?"

George shook his head at Terence who fought inwardly not to combat the being.

"This technology was a gift!"

"Enough!"

The Arenan's voice sent a shockwave through the command center. Technicians clutched their heads as blood seeped from their eyes, ears, and noses. Kevin fell to one knee, withstanding the onslaught. Even the second in command was only slightly affected by it.

"This planet will be cleansed."

He raised one hand in a prayer like gesture to his chest. Black pulsed from his body, flowing like liquid throughout the room. George shot forth, attempting to stop him from activating the power he was about to unleash. He knocked Terence down out of the way as he past her. A few feet from his target, George saw the Arenan's face contort deviously.

Darkness consumed Metropolis.

Smoke billowed from destroyed structures at the base of Mecca. The New Order had been pushed back and Heines's group formed a defensive line at every point around the facility. Part of the reason for the halt was the sky. So many reasons for the event went through Veronica's mind, fully aware that only aliens had such power. She walked over to the jagged edge of what used to be her office and surveyed the area outside.

"What a mess."

Alicia came up behind her. The lab coat and glasses were gone. There was blood splatter on her white shirt and smudges on her face.

"And we don't know if this is another alien attack."

"I think the Litigator did something."

"Oh," Alicia laughed. "I don't think so. This is not his aesthetic."

One of the guards came through the jagged opening that used to be a doorway. He walked briskly towards them, looking panicked.

"Professor," his voice came out rushed. "You need to get to the atrium."

The first thought that came in her head was her children who had been fighting the enemy down there. She spun around to face the guard.

"Are my children okay? Are they hurt?"

His face scrunched.

"They have a few minor wounds, nothing serious."

"Then what?" Veronica became irritated.

"You need to see it for yourself. I have guards on the ready in case it proves a threat."

Before Veronica could asked anymore questions, Alicia grabbed her by the forearm and started walking to the opening. She stopped when the guard didn't follow.

"Are you coming?"

Embarrassed by his lack of response, he joined them. As they entered the corridor, he took the lead as a precaution. There were still some enemy fighters inside determined to keep up the fight despite the new circumstances. They arrived in the nearly gutted atrium and found her son and daughter poised ready to strike along with four other guards surrounding a strange anomaly in the center of the area. It was a ghostly white, almost liquid as it shimmied like a glob. Then it stabilized into a ball, grew exponentially until it reached the floor, and turned black.

Without warning, a body shot out of the black hole and tumbled to the floor, landing face down.

Caleb moved in to strike.

"No, wait!" Veronica cried, hoping to stop his attack.

To her and everyone else's surprise he slid on his knees towards the person and helped them sit up. Xander raised his head and appeared to be in a daze as he slumped against his brother's chest.

"Hey!" His brother smacked one of his cheeks. "Snap out of it!"

Veronica covered her mouth with both hands. She turned to Alicia who stared at Xander warily. Christine went and sat in front of him.

"Here, let me try."

She raised her hand to deliver a heavy slap. Veronica felt her legs move and she was upon them, stopping her daughter's blow mid strike.

"Don't you dare," she hissed. Still holding on to her daughter's wrist, Veronica turned to the medical team treating the wounded further in. "Get a medic over here, now!"

"Let go of me!" Christine wrenched her arm free.

The medic came over and held the slim line body scanner over Xander, moving over him slowly to give the data time to compile. When he finished, the device beeped, and he looked over the results.

"I detect a few nanobytes lingering in his system making minor repairs. Looks like he suffered extensive damage. From my calculations, it must have taken days, possible weeks to recover. That's why there are still traces of it. He's not fully healed even though he appears to be from the outside."

"What happened to you?" Veronica knelt by him.

Caleb practically shielded Xander from her.

She frowned at him.

"What are you doing?"

"You were the one who sent him out there alone.

Now you want to act like he matters? You're the last person he needs to comfort him."

"And what about the two of you?" Veronica snapped. "Constantly bullying him made him feel what?"

"At least we paid attention to him!"

The medic scooted away, not wanting to get caught in the middle. Alicia let out a sigh of exasperation and started to walk towards them.

"Stop." It was barely a whisper yet Xander got their attention. "Please."

Xander was visibly exhausted. He struggled forward onto his knees. His body shook.

"Take it easy, you little shit." Caleb warned. "You're no super soldier."

Veronica caressed his face. He leaned into her touch.

"Can I get him to the medical bay?" The medic asked.

"Oh," Veronica removed her hand. "Of course."

"No time," Xander said.

Veronica's face became stern.

"What's going on out there? Is this the Litigator's fault?"

A small fighter craft landed on the atrium's exposed edge. Its thrusters cut out and the hatch opened. Professor Heines stepped out followed by three of his assistants. He wore a lab coat over his combat bodysuit. The impracticality of it bordered on absurd. Yet, it suited him.

"I would like to know as well. It looks like the end of days."

"Guardians," Xander breathed out.

"What? Guardians?" Veronica was confused.

"They're angry at the Litigator. Sky is from them showing up."

"Oh god," Alicia said softly. "What are we in for now?"

Xander managed to regain his composure and sat up straight.

"They had been watching. Galactic guardians. When the Litigator overstepped, they decided to intervene."

"What do these beings look like?" Heines asked.

"Angels. Like in the archives."

Their eyes went wide in disbelief. Caleb came out of his shock before the others and his eyes narrowed.

"How did you get here?"

Alicia perked up at that.

"Yes. You just appeared out of thin air. Are you really Xander Headland?"

That startled Veronica and she glared over at her as she started to go into a combat stance. Alicia gave her a warning look.

Xander simply nodded.

"I understand your trepidation. But, I am. They threw me in some sort of vortex. I," he shuddered, taking a breath. "Saw things in between space and time. Which makes no sense. I only moved from one place to another on the planet."

"It makes perfect sense," Heines stated. "Humans have yet to perfect teleportation. We are still so far behind our alien counterparts."

"Wait!" Veronica looked around then back at Xander. "Where are your companions? And the vehicle?"

"Left behind. There was no need for the vehicle to come back with me."

"But the data!"

Caleb stood and pointed down at her.

"See? That's the only thing she cared about in the first place."

Veronica also stood and confronted him.

"That's not true, and you know it!"

"Please!" Xander got to his feet with help from his sister. "There's no time."

"Why? What is it?"

Loud cracking filled the air and they all looked to the sky. Hot white lines spread in a crisscross pattern until blinding light shot forth blocking out the view before them. A beautiful being aglow in white robes descended towards them. White wings each one easily spanning six feet flapped twice, sending it down faster. As the being approach they saw it was a female. Her bronze skin complimented her jet-black hair and golden eyes. She hovered in the air beyond the atrium. Xander's eyes widened. She smiled at him.

"Arenan," Xander whispered.

"Good," her voice echoed all around them. "You are safely back where you belong."

Heines was rooted to the floor, slack jawed among the others. Veronica's assistant was unfazed. Instead Alicia positioned herself in front of Veronica and her children. The being's eyes intensified as she glowered over her nose at Alicia.

"And what will you do, human?"

Veronica's assistant suddenly became frightened as intense pressure pushed down on the area, bringing anyone not already on the floor to their knees then laid flat. It lasted only a few seconds. When everyone recovered, some cautiously getting back up, the Arenan's smile returned.

"This planet can no longer sustain life as it is. We have decided to fix it. To do that, all humans must be removed from its surface."

Veronica, still down sitting on her side propped up on her hands stared at the Arenan in horror. Alicia knelt by her.

"Screw that! Who are you to decide? You're just going

to wipe us out on a whim? That makes you no better than the Litigator!"

The Arenan looked down on them with pity. Her demeanor changed and Veronica could see the being had no more patience.

"This is our decree."

She raised one hand in a halting gesture and golden light spread from behind her, flowing to her hand. Veronica managed to lean forward; an arm stretched out.

"No! Wait!" Veronica screamed.

"Sleep." The Arenan deadpanned.

The golden light engulfed all of Mecca and everyone, friend and enemy fell.

REFUGE

Grannalt checked on Brody then met the others outside the vehicle. Bree stood deep in thought with his arms crossed. Fravral as usual didn't seem to have a care in the world. Seth had come out of the Cybok's pod citing the being had fallen into a deep sleep. Erin sat next to Gragor engrossed in his tales of battle. Stranded at the base of the hill exposed to the guardians, the group huddled together to brainstorm. Grannalt cleared his throat to get their attention.

"Not to bother you or anything, but the Arenans are planning to tear this place up. We need a plan to get off Earth."

Bree nodded, uncrossing his arms, and turned to Fravral.

"How capable is this ship to reach space? Preferably out of range to the nearest planet."

Fravral glanced up from the casing of food in his lap with a disinterested expression.

"If we had a decent navigation system and a sustainable power source, sure. This ship has been through hell. The fact that it still functions is beyond me."

Gragor stood, brushing the dirt form his suit.

"It surprised me as well. How do we remedy this situation?" He nodded at the hilltop. "They've already started."

They all stared at the sky now full of cracks spewing white light. Seth averted his gaze to the Relliant ship. He seemed to scrutinize it in a way that made Fravral uncomfortable. Seth pointed at the ship's upper deck.

"Can something dock into there?"

"What?" Fravral frowned.

Gragor started laughing then caught his breath.

"Good eye, kid. Yes. Something could dock there."

Grannalt became excited.

"Can said docked thing fully interface with the ship?"

"What are you all going on about?" Fravral was irritated not being in the loop.

Erin jumped up, beaming as she pointed to the vehicle.

"We can use her!"

Grannalt had a strange sensation of the AI tensing at the thought. He walked back and leaned into the front section.

"Could you do it? I know it's probably bigger than you're used to."

"That is not the issue," the AI answered.

"Then explain."

"Vessel is classified hostile. Interfacing would cause resistance from its end."

"Are you saying my ship is being uncooperative?" Fravral asked.

"Correct." The AI's voice seemed to huff.

Grannalt wondered how much nuance was built into her personality's learning capability.

"Well, you're going to have to try and get along. This is a do or die situation. I don't want to be removed," Grannalt brought his fingers up in quotations. "Understand?"

"Please stand clear." The AI instructed.

He stepped away from the vehicle per its request

and the hatch sealed. Gragor made a concerned face.

"Shouldn't your son be taken out first?"

Grannalt cocked his head then shrugged.

"I assume she would have said something if it were an issue."

The vehicle lifted off the ground. Bree turned to Fravral and raised his brow. Fravral set the food to the side and went to his ship. Inside the cockpit he initialized the systems and pushed the button that would open the top section of the ship. The vehicle slowly did a one hundred eighty-degree curve so that it could glide into the docking area. The group watched in awe as the vehicle fit perfectly into the Relliant ship. With a loud clink, both vessels were merged.

"Attempting interface." The vehicle AI announced.

Warning lights flooded the cockpit. Fravral shook his head.

"My ship doesn't like her."

"Then make it like her," Gragor said angrily.

"I'll try."

"Warning. Hostile entity attempting full control of operations." The ship's AI system came online. "Rejecting secondary host."

"Input override sequence. Code…"

"Override command denied."

Fravral sat back stunned. He looked over at Gragor. Grannalt sighed and addressed the vehicle.

"Invasive protocol. Stealth assimilation. Make him submit."

"That's a bit harsh," Gragor said.

"No time for this foolishness," Bree added. He looked at the vehicle. "Make it quick."

"Command accepted. Initiating stealth infiltration mode."

One by one, the warning lights started to shut off.

Fravral appeared disappointed.

"How long until you learn the system?" Grannalt asked the vehicle AI.

"Approximately thirty-four hours."

"Plenty of time." Gragor paced the small clearing. "I say it would take a while for the Arenans to clear the planet."

"We'll be long gone before that." Bree agreed.

"I feel kind of bad," Erin said, pouting. They stared at her. "I mean, we're just running away again, right. Leaving everyone else behind."

"I want to live." Seth declared it so simply they were all taken aback by its delivery. "Let's get away from here."

While they waited for the interfacing to be complete, the group kept a close vigil on the Litigator and the two Arenans opening pathways for their associates. Already, the valley seemed unusually still. There was no sound coming from anywhere even though they knew there were New Order people nearby.

They're scared. Gragor concluded. They had every right to be.

"Merge complete." The AI's voice broke him and the others out of their reverie.

To their astonishment, the ship began to reconfigure so that the vehicle created a secondary bridge. The Cybok's pod was separated from the tow and attached underneath. Gragor blinked a few times to make sure he wasn't seeing things.

Grannalt slapped him on the back.

"All aboard."

Fravral was in the cockpit marveling at the different options on the command screen. Directly above was the vehicle's front section, the bottom opened for easy access.

"Let's get this show started." He engaged the engines then looked up. "You taking it from here?"

"Absolutely," the AI replied.

The thrusters ignited and the ship rose into the air. As it came within the same level as the Litigator and the Arenans, the group turned to see them. The Litigator gave them an encouraging grin. The Arenans paid them no mind. Tilting backwards, the thrusters let out a blast, shooting the ship through the stratosphere and into orbit.

Gragor watched Grannalt's body relax in the upper deck as if he was glad to be in space. Then it hit him. Grannalt never wanted to be on Earth. He was a fighter who was probably always on a ship. To have been grounded for so long must have been hard on him. He caught Seth also staring at Grannalt. A sense of sadness came over the young man. Gragor felt Seth understood his mother.

The engines reduced power and the ship went at a steady pace. Debris cluttered Earth's orbit and continued farther out. Relliant ships, broken, abandoned, floated in the darkness. Gragor's heart sank. This was not how he wanted the battle to go.

Damn it, Tartha!

He glanced up and caught Grannalt's gaze. The two rival aliens had an unspoken agreement. The fight between their races, as far as they were concerned, was over.

FAREWELL, TERRA

The first Arenan stepped off the hilltop and hovered in the air, their body rotating slowly while surveying the landscape and horizon. They connected with their counterparts and the ground began to shake across the globe. Every living being on the planet, alien and humanoid, was in a deep slumber oblivious to the chaos around them.

At Mecca, the Arenan collected all the bodies outside the main building and moved them inside. They waved one hand and a thin layer of frost formed on them. The shield that once protected the facility shrunk until it only encompassed the main structure. As the Arenan's arms raised up, so did Mecca. In the wake of its ascension, the ground tore apart and the small surrounding city, now deserted, crumbled into the gaping holes. Mecca hovered midair in direct sight of the Arenan.

The sky opened as if being peeled back and bright light beamed out of the crack. Mecca was lifted up and disappeared through it. The Arenan stared down at the carnage still ongoing below. Buildings, streets, and bridges all collapsed into the abyss. Satisfied with the results, the Arenan drifted off to join their counterpart.

Metropolis proved tricky for the Arenan who lingered after cloaking it in darkness. He grimaced at the sheer size of the five-sector facility. The slightest movement created an earthquake and the low tide swelled higher than anticipated. Determined to dislodge it quickly, he forced it up with a jerk of his arms and watched in disgust as the entire region churned. Another Arenan came to his side and observed the situation.

"I had a similar issue with the place known as Facility Three."

"That one is smaller than this!" The Arenan spat. "Look at what it's done so far."

"We are here to terraform this planet," the other said matter of fact.

"This is more work than I care to do."

Metropolis finally rose up exposing its underbelly and the two Arenans stare at it in awe. Lining the bottom and sides was a complex structure of purple lights. They pulsed as if alive. And they were. The Arenan seethed at it and turned to the other.

"Organics!"

The other Arenan floated closer to inspect Metropolis and tilted his head.

"Then they will help us."

He sent a telepathic message to the one on the hilltop.

"Cresnia needs to assist us. He cannot refuse."

The Arenan on the hilltop frowned as the visual of Metropolis was sent in his mind. He reached out into the solar system and found the Organic ship sitting on the outskirts. Cresnia appeared to be waiting. The Arenan flew out to space and floated before it.

"You have a remedy?" The Arenan asked.

Cresnia, the Organic creature navigating the giant ship, smiled.

"I do. A shame you put them all to sleep. I would have taken them." His eyes glowed. "Of course, we'd have to kill them first."

The Arenan gave him a sinister stare.

"That is not an option. We need to get them in orbit and away from here."

Cresnia seemed to pout.

"As you wish."

Beams of lavender light shot out from the ship and hit Metropolis. The Arenan rose the facility further into the stratosphere as the beams started to create a new structure around it. Metropolis was being reconfigured faster than it rose. By the time it entered space, the giant sector resembled a ship similar in design as the Organic's. A shield concaved on both sides until it covered the entire thing.

The Arenan adjourned at the hilltop and watched all the beings leaving Earth. When the last one disappeared in the sky, the first Arenan turned to Roland.

"Now you can rain destruction on this place as much as you want. Once that is out of your system, a creator will be sent."

Roland glanced up at them puzzled.

"The original creator is not coming to fix his work?" Roland asked.

The Arenan frowned.

"The original creator abandoned this planet long ago. Another can do better."

The Arenans drifted backwards from him and left the planet. With their departure, the sky turned a shade of orange, letting in the sun. Roland stood on the hilltop. Angry at the chain of events, he did as they expected. The Book of Litigation reappeared, this time glowing a dark amber color. Multiple super storms spread across the planet, destroying everything in its wake.

Within days the sky went dark and ash began to flow. The Earth's core leaked molten lava into its veins. On the tenth day his anger started to wane, and he decided to end it quickly. With one final force of energy, he brought Terra to her knees.

From his ship, Cresnia watched the newly configured Metropolis' thrusters send it out towards Saturn. The other sectors were scattered not far away from them. His eyes darkened, not caring for Roland's last act. He stayed to witness the planet's last moments.

Such a waste.

A dark spot appeared on the southern hemisphere and grew across the planet, an indication of everything dying. Earth sat, a ball of black and brown.

Its vibrance gone.

~END~

ABOUT THE AUTHOR

Hi there. I'm Maquel A. Jacob. I have had a passion for the written word since the age of seven, reading everything I could get my grubby little hands on which included encyclopedias and the thesaurus. At twelve, I had my first encounter with a Stephen King novel and was hooked. I then became inspired to write my own brand of fiction. Combining multiple genres to keep things interesting.

I am a HUGE Anime fan, love a great bottle of wine and rock out to heavy metal music. Green and lush Oregon is where I currently reside spinning imaginary worlds in my head and daydreaming.

For cool limited-edition Swag, updates, FREE short stories, Newsletters

...and more

Visit: http://www.majacobauthor.com/

Like Maquel A. Jacob on Facebook

Follow on Twitter @MaquelAJ1

Also find me on Goodreads

MAJart Works on Instagram